I0620809

CABO CAPER

CABO CAPER

R. LAWSON

The characters and events portrayed in this book are fictitious. Any similarity to real persons, living or dead, is coincidental and not intended by the author.

Text copyright © 2013 R. Lawson

All rights reserved.
Printed in the United States of America.
No part of this book may be reproduced, or stored in a retrieval system, or transmitted in any form or by any means, electronic, mechanical, photocopying, recording, or otherwise, without express written permission of the publisher.

ISBN-13: 978-0-9898916-0-8

DEDICATION

To Chips – ILYYT

EPIGRAPH

"Every dog has his day,
 and a good dog
 might have two days."
-Johnny Copeland from <u>Vineland</u> by Thomas Pychon

TABLE OF CONTENTS

CHAPTER ONE

VACATION IN BAJA

"Biff! Biff! Come quickly! They've got Boo!" his wife yelled in alarm.

Biff Roberts had just finished his morning shower, wiped the steam off the mirror, and started shaving. He responded rapidly, grabbing his .9 mm Beretta from the holster hanging on the bathroom doorknob. He ran immediately to their suite's balcony overlooking the Sea of Cortez, and the SE corner of the parking lot of the posh resort.

His wife, Mary Beth, hysterically pointed in the direction of the parking lot 80 yards away. There, three scruffy Mexicans were dragging their 14 year old son kicking and screaming towards a beat-up VW combi van in the far corner of the lot. Boo was putting up a frantic fight, resisting his abductors. Unfortunately, he was no match for the burly Mexicans who overpowered him.

Biff spotted Boo's surfboard abandoned by the edge of the beach pathway adjoining the parking lot. Moments earlier Boo had caught a nice wave off the Zippers reef, surfing it perfectly for 100 yards to shore, a thrilling experience on his trimester break from prep school. Now he was engaged in a terrifying fight for his life.

At the sound of a woman's scream, early morning diners on the breakfast terrace of the posh resort rushed to the rails to witness the sudden disturbance. Shocked, they were aghast at the kidnapping unfolding before them. They were paralyzed in a state of inaction.

How could this possibly occur at this famous Cabo resort noted for its beauty and serenity?

"Look up there! That man has a gun!" one tourist shouted, pointing to Biff standing at his balcony's edge. The crowd's focus shifted in that direction, spotting a large blonde American wearing only boxer shorts, with shaving cream all over his face. He was pointing a pistol at the three Mexican abductors. The man's wife was crying and screaming, "Stop them!" hysterically.

A sudden shock wave surged though the tourists who had come to Cabo for fun and frolic, not this graphic violence.

The vacationer's warning was no sooner spoken when a shot rang out from the balcony. The terrified crowd scattered, ducking for cover. They heard a yell of pain from the parking lot instantly.

Biff's shot hit one of the kidnappers in the shoulder, spinning him around. The wounded man grimaced and cursed. The other two culprits came to his rescue. They quickly and roughly tossed Boo through the van's sliding side door. The driver revved up the engine.

"Jesus Christo!", the injured abductor cursed as he jumped in behind Boo.

The patrons in the restaurant pavilion remained under cover, fearing more gunshots. This scene was not part of their package deal. Certainly not the 'pina colada scene' in the hotel's glossy advertisement. They shivered in anticipation of what would happen next?

"Dammit! I can't see well." The morning sun had melted Biff's shaving cream, inadvertently seeping into his left eye impairing his depth perception. The cream stung. Biff squinted, handicapped by essentially monocular vision. He had to avoid hitting his son with his second shot. Usually Biff was quite accurate at this range.

"Gotta be careful..." He took aim, squeezing out a second shot, shattering the van's rear window with a loud concussion of crashing glass. The van lurched, spinning out on the loose gravel and pebbles. Tires squealed. The combi swerved wildly, almost out of control.

"Oh my God!" the stunned crowd gasped, "What next?" they thought.

Biff readied his third shot "Gotta get a tire with this one." The van was about 100 yards away, approaching the exit, as Biff fired his third round.

"Missed! Hit the bumper, Dammit! They'll be on the ocean highway in minutes. The bastards are getting away!"

CHAPTER TWO
CABO SURF RESORT

"**W**hat a way to start a vacation! What am I going to do now?"

Biff uncharacteristically fretted and returned to his suite to console his sobbing wife. He had to get a grip on this unexpected, bizarre circumstance suddenly thrust upon them, a maddening experience beyond the pale.

Mary Beth was inconsolable. She was devastated. Speechless, she could not stop crying. No words could comfort her grief, or describe what she was suffering through; witnessing the abduction of their son, Boo. Biff hugged her tightly, long and hard. He felt her pain, sorrow, and loss. He regretted that his intervention in the kidnapping had failed. He must come up with a rescue plan.

But first, he must collect his thoughts. It was not his nature to become rattled. Maintaining his composure and making accurate decisions were his hallmark. This trait saved his life and others on past occasions. Biff relied on his self confidence that he'd figure out a plan.

They arrived late last night on an Aero México flight from San Francisco, too late to rent a car. Biff Roberts' company allowed him to squeeze in a few days of vacation at the Cabo Surf resort before setting out on his latest consulting mission with their Mexican counterparts. The critical mission was highly classified.

Biff figured spending the trimester Winter Break with his son, home from prep school, and his wife in Cabo would be relaxing before he attended to his business. The weather would be perfect for Boo to surf and unwind after a miserable winter in Boston. He regretted that their daughter, Caroline, couldn't join them. She had late winter training in Phoenix with the ASU softball team. She was their star pitcher. Biff understood. He'd missed several late winter breaks when he pitched at Yale. He was proud of her and regretted she could not join them.

Mary Beth had stopped sobbing, but appeared visibly shaken. Biff seized the opportunity to analyze this predicament with her.

"Honey, if the flight had been on time last night, we could have rented a car instead of taking a taxi. I could have chased after those bastards!"

She recognized her husband's dilemma. He had a reputation as a "man of action". She shared his frustrations. The fact that they lacked a car was little consolation to her. She knew Biff instinctively would have pursued the abductors, if he had a vehicle.

She had faith in him. Thirty years of marriage reinforced her belief that he'd come up with a solution. She was amazed how Biff always came through against huge odds, but Boo's kidnapping might prove an insurmountable probability for even a man of his extraordinary capabilities. She witnessed one of his incredible accomplishments just last year in Phoenix when their daughter's boyfriend mysteriously disappeared. Biff remarkably recovered him with the help of the FBI after a series of bizarre twists and turns. Ironically, now their son had been abducted! The stakes had been raised to a very personal level within hours of their arrival.

She was pale and trembling. Biff went to her side, hugged her and kissed her forehead. "I'm so sorry, dear. I'll call my colleague over at our consulate. Serge will help us."

She grasped his hand tightly, Biff had valuable contacts. He'd come through. She was convinced they'd find Boo. She dared not to think otherwise. The alternative was unbearable. She must shut that negative thought out, stay positive, and be brave.

Before Biff could place the call to the US Consulate, the doorbell rang loudly. The front door was open. They saw a well dressed gentleman standing politely at the balcony entrance, hesitant to interrupt their conversation considering the dire circumstances. It was an awkward moment. Courteously he awaited the guests' acknowledgement.

Nervously, he introduced himself as he sensed their questioning gaze resting upon him.

"I'm Andres Delarosa, the resort manager. Words cannot express our regrets in this unfortunate incident. I assure you it is unprecedented at our resort. We'll do everything possible to find your son and apprehend the perpetrators."

He appeared sincere, Biff reflected.

"I've called the police, they are on the way. My staff is taking statements from witnesses. How may we assist you during this trying situation? Nothing like this has ever happened before! Our security has always been vigilant. Top notch. I don't understand how this happened. I apologize."

He blurted out this apology sympathetically, obviously quite upset.

Biff's mind churned, preoccupied with other concerns, formulating a "game plan" He allowed the manager to express his grief and apologies without interruption. His mind raced on 'fast forward', focused on a plan of action to rescue Boo.

The manager continued, ignoring Biff's apparent disinterest.

"Did you get a license number, Mr. Roberts?"

"The van's plates were dirty, impossible to get a number, but it definitely was a Baja plate on an old beat up VW van."

He could hear his wife sobbing in their bedroom where she'd sought solitude. She didn't want to talk with anyone, just resigned to let Biff handle it.

"May I enquire why you have a gun in your possession, Sir?", he asked politely. "It's illegal in Mexico, especially for foreigners."

"I have a special permit. The reason I do is classified", Biff replied dismissively.

"Must be some kind of international 'big shot," the manager thought. "I won't go there. The authorities certainly will. This fellow seems self assured. He's had a rough day. Despite the circumstances, this American could be in for big trouble."

"I understand how upset you must be, but I hope you will cooperate with the police investigation."

Biff just nodded, retrieving his laptop computer, hoping for a WIFi connection.

Mary Beth returned to the living room, and sat quietly on the sofa, wiping tears from her eyes.

The manager immediately noted the contrast in their emotions, faced with a family crisis. Señor Roberts remained unusually calm and collected, a bit preoccupied, detached. Most people in this situation would be apoplectic. He'd hate to be in this American's shoes. He'd be going nuts!

"Somehow, this American maintains his composure, focused on something other than the moment."

The manager glanced across the room at the wife, trembling on the couch. Tearful, pale, anxious, on the verge of losing it. Personally, he knew of nothing more stressful and traumatic than the loss of a child, either by death or kidnapping with its prolonged uncertainty. She desperately strived to hold it together, at lost or words or action.

Seemingly ignoring the manager's remarks regarding the police, Biff abruptly changed the subject.

"Do you have WIFI or cable on the premises?" tinkering with his plug- in equipment.

"Yes sir. WIFI in all the suites. It's preferable to cell phones. We experience a lot of dropped calls. The reception is sketchy. E-mails are a far more reliable form of communication on the Baja Peninsula."

"If you will excuse me, I must contact a professional Mexican colleague immediately. Thank you for coming by to check on us and offering your services", Biff said as he booted up his specially coded laptop computer.

"Let me know if you need anything", the manager offered as he exited the door.

"Thank you. We will not hesitate", Biff replied. He was busy organizing his E-mail, never looking up to acknowledge the manager's departure.

As the manager returned to his office, he recounted his exchange with this imposing American.

"Big strong guy, fit for his age. His behavior came across as a bit strange. His son had just been kidnapped. He'd fired three shots at the assailants, wounding one. Now he can't wait to get on his computer to contact a colleague? What's that all about? These Americans, sometimes I just don't know! Que sera sera!"

Biff went over and shut the door. His wife had returned to the bed-room and resumed crying, lying on the bed, her face buried in a pillow. She was absolutely emotionally spent … At the end of her emotional rope.

"Hang in there, dear. I'm contacting my friend. He'll help us get Boo back, I promise." He gently patted her shoulder, attempting to reassure her.

"I hope and pray so, Biff", she moaned without looking up.

Biff returned to his laptop and punched out an urgent E-mail.

To: Serge Betancourt

> U.S. CONSULATE
> CABO SAN LUCAS, MEXICO
> FROM: B.C.ROBERTS V
> U.S. CONSULATE, SF

Serge-Big problem! Three Mexicans kidnapped our son about 15 min-utes ago. If you hurry over to the Cabo Surf, I'll fill in the sordid details.

Need your help urgently. No car. Cell phone unreliable. Arrived late last night just in time for this RF! Biff

CHAPTER THREE
U.S. CONSULATE – CABO SAN LUCAS

"**A**nother cup of coffee, Señor Betancourt?", asked his lovely secretary, Alicia Nicascio.

Serge Betancourt was conflicted. He didn't know which he looked more forward to each morning, his strong Mexican brew, or the sight of his petite, attractive secretary.

She was a snappy dresser with a great complexion, trim young figure, engaging personality, and somewhat intelligently inclined. And, she could type 100 words a minute. What more could he ask for? He thought about that for a few seconds...

"Oh, to be young again!", he mischievously fantasized...

Serge was now 55 years old, a bit out of shape, twice divorced with three kids who hadn't called or written him a single letter in the last 3 years. He loathed exercise. He ate too much, drank too much, smoked too much, and swore too much.

Serge was profane, but not vulgar, if that distinction can be made. He favored the profanity "fuck", used as a noun, verb, or adjective. As in "F.U. and the horse you rode in on", or "F.U., strong letter to follow!"

These friendly putdowns always elicited a good laugh, often defusing a tense situation. He was not a mean person, just very direct and brashly straightforward in his relationships. No B.S. Once you understood Serge's behavior in that context, you were not offended.

Actually, most of the staff at the consulate found his approach refreshing. No question where you stood with Serge. No bureaucratic 'double speak', or 'posturing'. You always got the straight answer.

Serge lived a lonely personal life, a series of "one night stands", but enjoyed no "significant other" relationship. His professional life was another matter.

Serge thrived at his profession, respected by the consulate staff. Despite his personal shortcomings, he faithfully performed his duties at the consulate flawlessly.

Although Serge represented a contradiction of accepted norms to maintain good health, he always passed his annual physical with flying colors.

"Good genes," he joked with a chuckle. No one was about to replace him. His stellar track record in the Cabo posting assured him of tenure. The local lifestyle wasn't all that bad either. In fact, it appealed to him.

He once tried to grow a beard to look like Ernest Hemingway. Unfortunately, he ended up looking like Dorian Gray.

"So much for that mid-life crisis, time to move on", he reflected after this last disappointment in a long series of setbacks.

While Serge had every reason in the world to be grumpy, he somehow maintained a positive outlook. He enjoyed a pleasant relationship with his colleagues, often cheery. His secretary, Alicia adored her boss.

After indulging in his thoughts and sipping his coffee, he addressed Alicia, who was waiting patiently for his instructions.

"Delicious coffee. Muchas gracias, Alicia. Any messages?" a perfunctory question.

It was Saturday morning, a half day at the consulate. Nothing ever happens on Saturday morning. Maybe Saturday night, if an American tourist got into some serious trouble, but not Saturday morning. Serge planned to go fishing in a couple of hours. Dorados were running big time.

"Yes Sir. This E-mail just arrived moments ago. It looks urgent. I printed it for you."

She spoke acceptable English with a soft Spanish accent. She awaited her boss' response.

Serge quickly read Biff's message. "Oh my God!" he uttered.

His pulse pounded with excitement in response to the incredible occurrence that Biff relayed in the E-mail. He'd not expected Biff's arrival until next week. Now this unimaginable abduction of his colleague's boy! Incredible!

This was tranquil Cabo, not Mexico City. This event was unprecedented!

Alicia observed the abrupt change in his demeanor. He had that "serious business" look on his face...Something big was about to happen.

"Alicia, I'll need my car and two bodyguards in five minutes. I'll be in and out of the office all weekend, so please be available by your cell phone. OK? I have some very important, unexpected business to attend to. Guard the fort."

"Yes sir", she respectfully replied, turning to return to her office. She didn't understand the expression "guard the fort", but she understood something very important happened. She'd hold all his calls until he returned.

Serge retrieved his service Glock from the locked desk drawer. He maintained a spartan office with everything in its proper place. Outside his chaotic family and private life, he was organized, if not compulsive. Everything professional was conducted habitually, with no deviations or variations. This practice limited errors, common mistakes, and misunderstandings. All critical attributes that his job demanded to attain consistent high performance. Serge was up to the task.

This one involved a challenging personal twist, however.

"Buenos dias, Carlos. Como se va, Armando?" Serge greeted his trusted bodyguards in the consulate's parking lot.

"Muy bien, y tu?" they responded. "Que pasa?" What's happening?

They enjoyed their boss' Spanish language endeavors. They encouraged him, in fact. He was improving, "mejor."

"Where we off to, boss?" Carlos enquired as they jumped in the Jeep Grand Cherokee. The bodyguards kept the white vehicle spotless, shining it frequently. It was their pride and joy.

"Cabo Surf", Serge replied, somewhat distractedly.

He pondered the alarming implications, thinking ahead about Biff's urgent message. Biff's high position in the company commanded maximum effort and support in this dire emergency. He couldn't imagine being in Biff's shoes.

"WTF!", he thought to himself. Except for a Christmas card four years ago from one daughter, all three of his kids could have been kidnapped as far as he knew.

The blare of a loud horn jolted his thoughts as Carlos slapped on his brakes to avoid T-boning an old, mud covered pickup truck recklessly running a red light at a busy intersection. The gritty farmer driving the truck angrily swore out his window, as if it was Carlos' fault. He was on a tirade, waving wildly out the window, turning the air blue.

As Carlos hit his brakes and swerved, a crate of the farmer's chickens careened over the pickup's open flatbed. The crate ricocheted off a car's hood, and crashed on the roadbed, scattering confused poultry everywhere, creating a chaotic traffic jam, and general mayhem.

Carlos flipped the furious farmer the "bird", then skillfully maneuvered through the jam like the race car driver he once was. He inadvertently ran over two birds while attempting to avoid running over a traffic cop. Close call! The hassled cop alertly jumped out of the way, yelling obscenities in Carlos' wake. No time to jot down a license, Carlos swerved once more and was gone!

Carlos sped off, laughing, enroute to the ocean highway north to Cabo Surf. He glanced in the rear view mirror.

"How you doing back there, Boss?"

Serge shifted nervously in his seat, but he said nothing. He was familiar with Carlos' driving skills. "Fortunately, he hadn't killed anyone yet."

"Carlos probably will be a bullfighter in his next life," Serge reflected.

Baja basked in a balmy morning. As they reached the ocean highway, Serge watched the sun glisten across the sea's white caps, as 10 knots of easterly breeze flickered across the water's surface.

Fishing boats headed north, up the Sea of Cortez to reap the day's bounty. Serge reflected. Normally, he would have been aboard, listening to the crackle of the "ship to shore" radio announcing a school of Dorado or pez bella in a couple of hours from now, if this emergency had not come up. Today he'd miss the fishermen's jokes, and probably for awhile until this serious problem was resolved.

Serge's thoughts returned to the problem at hand. "Who would kidnap Biff's kid? Was it just a random event? The motive…?"

Serge took nothing at face value. He had expected Biff to arrive next week to consult on their upcoming joint mission.

"Guess he was trying to squeeze in some family time. Wonder why he didn't notify me of his plans?"

Many Americans visited Cabo during Winter and Spring Breaks. Wish Biff had given me a 'heads up'. I would have detailed a security team to meet them at the airport, and look after them so they could enjoy Cabo's good life… "All fun and games… "Like the Jimmy Buffet lyric 'changes in latitude, changes in attitude."

Serge ran through his mental list of 'woulda, couldas'. "WTF! Too late now!"

Serge's thoughts returned to evaluating the kidnap scenarios, trying to piece it all together. He considered various angles and ramifications enroute to meet up with Biff at Cabo Surf. He could not piece the puzzle all together. Too complex!

"This will require some profound thought. A concerted effort with Biff and his colleagues."

It was difficult to concentrate with Carlos speeding around curves of the ocean highway. There were no guard rails to avoid a one hundred foot drop-off into the jagged rocks or sea below. Carlos weaved in and out of traffic on the two lane road. Drivers saw him coming in their rear view mirrors, lights blinking, the colorful consulate flag on the bumper flying.

Considerately and wisely, they gave way. Good decision. Carlos would have cut them off otherwise.

They reached their destination in record time. The resort guards recognized the consulate flag and waved them through. Carlos slowed the pace down through the winding driveway, lined by bougainvillea and tall palms. The entrance was impressive, Serge observed.

As they approached the parking lot, Serge noticed the local police had already cordoned off a large part of the lot near the beach with yellow tape, the typical crime scene.

At the far end he recognized Biff Roberts talking, and pointing in an animated fashion with the chief investigator.

"Tall American, athletic build, thick blond hair, couldn't miss him. Biff Roberts towered over the local police."

"It will be interesting to see how he wiggles out of this jam, considering they have no idea of his identity," Serge mused.

"My pal may be in big time trouble with the Mexican authorities."

"How's Biff going to explain his Beretta? Firing three shots?"

"Would he blow his cover one week before their joint mission? Let's see how resourceful he is. Can Biff live up to his reputation?"

Like Serge, Biff was a 30 plus year CIA field officer under diplomatic cover. He was experienced in managing difficult situations like this.

CHAPTER FOUR
THE CRIME SCENE –
SATURDAY MORNING

The police definitely were not happy with Biff at all. While they sympathized regarding his son's abduction, they were vigorously interrogating him. Biff's actions raised some serious questions demanding some serious answers. They were getting 'heavy' in their interrogation.

"Why did you have a pistol? Where did you get it? Tell us why you thought you had the authority to shoot a Mexican citizen? That was a brazen act, Señor. Illegal, even though they were absconding with your son, unfortunately."

They fired one question after another, at first not giving Biff time to answer or explain.

"You fired three shots. Didn't you realize you were endangering the resorts' guests? What's your problem, cowboy? You are a loose canon!"

They informed him repeatedly that it was "muy importante" for him to answer their questions. To cooperate.

The tough police sergeant continued grilling Biff who remained cool, calm, and collected. He patiently waited his turn to clarify matters. He was prepared to defend his actions in English or Spanish. Biff spoke Spanish fluently. He'd spent five years in Salvador and Nicaragua during the Sandinista- Contra conflict. He understood how these Latin Americans behaved, especially in their interrogation protocol. It was important not to interrupt them, argue, or become confrontational.

"No need to aggravate them. It just made matters worse."

Biff remained focused on rescuing his son, not these yahoos' interrogation. Frankly, he didn't give a rat's ass about what they considered "importante". To him, Boo was the only thing he considered "importante" at this point.

Finally, the officers granted Biff an opportunity to explain his actions.

He was persuasive, cool in his presentation of the facts, but evasive regarding his personal circumstances, confusing his interrogators with crafty, ambiguous answers. Biff mastered equivocation, alternating between fluent Spanish and English, further confusing the Mexican officers. He never gave them a straight answer. He chose his words carefully, with veiled references and diversions, purposely deceiving them.

"Who the Hell is this hombre?" the police sergeant asked himself. "What's his story?"

He was becoming frustrated with this gringo. "Why can't he answer a simple question without digressions? Jesus Christo!"

Realizing he was running out of verbal ploys, and sensing their increasing displeasure at his answers, Biff took another tack to stall until Serge arrived. He needed some convincing cover that Serge would surely deliver.

Meanwhile, he reached into his pocket, retrieving his diplomatic passport. Politely, he showed it to them, carefully guarding his reason for being in Mexico, despite their probing questions. This established his status as 'a person of importance'.

Their attitude changed, becoming more in deference. They had no clue regarding his covert status. Actually, Biff was cleverly controlling his predicament with his polished savoir-faire.

Adroitly, he maneuvered himself into a neutral position, if not a commanding one, in this interaction. He could sense the sergeant was losing his patience, but now reluctant to press too aggressively.

"Maybe I should back off," the sergeant thought. "This guy can handle our pressure."

The idea that Biff didn't represent the usual American tourist started to sink in.

"This hombre is some kind of big shot. Carrying an official diplomatic passport. Could have a lot of political ramifications."

"Do I want to get too deeply involved with this? I could be embroiled for months. Better rethink this. It's bad enough already, no need to further complicate matters. I can't get a sensible answer out of this guy anyway. He's shifty."

That was the status of the situation when Serge and his bodyguards arrived on the scene.

Biff greeted them with his signature grin, as if implying, "About time!"

Serge immediately noted that even in the midst of a family tragedy, Biff somehow maintained his presence. He had mastered self-command in the face of adversity. In fact, some considered him an artist in manners and deportment. Stress represented only a facet in life's challenges. The measure of a man was to accept the challenge, and overcome it.

Serge immediately picked up on Biff's subliminal message, relayed by 'the characteristic grin.'

Serge smiled and rapidly assumed command, in a natural, pleasant manner, not the least bit officious or offending.

Biff picked up on this, "pretty smooth!"

"Good to see ya, Biff", shaking his hand vigorously, and giving him a warm, sincere 'abrazo', customary in Mexico among good friends.

"How's the Lone Ranger? Glad you got here, Serge. It was getting a bit dicey. Glad you got my smoke signal."

The sergeant observed this warm exchange, thinking to himself, "Made the correct decision in 'backing off.' This gringo is indeed some kind of big shot, if Serge welcomes him in that manner. Serge is a straight shooter, a 'buen hombre'. I lucked out."

Serge quickly repeated this Latino formality with the somewhat chastened sergeant, indicating to Biff that this 'sticky wicket' was about to be resolved amicably.

"Hola, Roberto. Coma está? Señor Roberts is an invited guest of our consulate, consulting on classified national business. I'm sure you understand Mr. Roberts has diplomatic immunity while here to assist us in a secret investigation. I'm certain you grasp the international ramifications of his son's abduction and will spare no effort in recovering his son and bring the kidnappers to justice."

Biff noted that Serge concisely laid it all out for the local authorities, 'This is how it is…'

Impressive performance. Serge had a lot of moxie. It was obvious to all that Serge was "the big dog in the fight". He had established an admirable reputation on the Baja peninsula. Today was 'payback'.

Serge glanced at Boo's surfboard by the pathway to the beach. On it sat a small glass jar containing the fragmented .9 mm bullet, presumably Biffs'. Both were labeled as "EXHIBITS" in large letters.

"Looks like Roberto's boys are hopping on the job."

"They're all over it… and me."

"Let me handle this, big fellow, OK?"

Over on the resort's terrace the tourists looked on with intense curiosity, captivated by the horrific drama of the morning's kidnapping and shootout. Hollywood could not have scripted it with anymore excitement. Now, what would happen next?

The police were questioning the tall blond American aggressively, until three official appearing gentlemen arrived. It seemed the new arrivals out ranked the local police. They were already defusing the situation that was becoming a bit testy.

Although, most of the onlookers conceded among themselves, that they were impressed with the American's restraint under such duress, before the three well dressed men arrived. Despite the fact his son was dragged away less than one hour ago, before his own eyes, and that he shot one of the assailants, this man was holding his own without losing his composure, as the police pounded him with a barrage of questions. The mornings' exciting encounter sparked immense interest in the kidnapping.

"This dude's cool," one commented.

"I'm really impressed," another tourist replied.

"Can you imagine what he and his wife are going through? Must be unbearable!"

"I don't even want to think about it! This whole thing is unreal, man!"

Several other mesmerized vacationers were on their Blackberry's, busily messaging home, relating the bizarre events of this morning:

"This will blow you away, dude…"

"No fuckin' way you can imagine the shit happening here in Cabo!…"

"You won't believe this, man…I'm not kidding!…"

"Hey! You'll never guess what just happened here in Cabo…"

"Holy shit! Wait 'til I tell you what just came down at our resort…"

"WTF! Wait until I tell you this mind-blowing story, guys…"

"On our first day of vacation here, some Mexicans kidnapped an American kid, igniting a gunfight, incredible!"

An L.A. scriptwriter busily scribbled notes on his napkin, ideas for a movie or TV show. He couldn't have dreamed this up this spontaneous drama.

"You wouldn't believe this, if you hadn't seen it yourself. Fabulous material!" he elated to the starlet accompanying him. "Right out of the blue!"

Meanwhile, Serge continued laying it on. "Our national mission is quite dangerous," he whispered into Roberto's ear. "That explains why Señor Roberts is armed. I hope you will keep this information confidential, Roberto. No one must know."

Roberto nodded his acknowledgement, flattered to share a national secret.

Serge backed away, then spoke for general consumption.

"You can understand the circumstances, and Señor Roberts' natural instinct to fire on his son's abductors. I'm sure you would have acted the same way if you were visiting Disneyland with your son and some thug attempted to snatch him, right, Roberto?"

"You betcha, Roberto!" Serge answered his own question that he'd directed to the sergeant.

The officer appeared a bit over whelmed by this tense Saturday morning crime investigation, definitely out of the ordinary for him. He feared getting in over his head.

Actually, Roberto appeared relieved that Serge showed up. "It may have saved his ass." Biff observed.

Serge's statement seemed to placate the investigative squad. Serge presented a convincing argument. "Difficult to disagree with his reasoning", they thought.

"Very persuasive, smooth move", Biff mused.

"I don't see any need for further questioning, do you, Roberto? I'll take full responsibility for this case, relieving you of the chore of explaining this awkward circumstance to your 'jefe.' Is that agreeable with you?"

The sergeant thought for a moment. "This is a good way to bail out of this complicated case. There have been no kidnappings in Cabo's history, that I can recall, much less a shooting at the elite Cabo Surf resort. This indeed is a complex case. I probably shouldn't get committed to a case that might cost me my job, if things go awry."

"OK, Serge. You've got a deal. We'll pursue the culprits, post an APB and assist you in any way we can. You'll have our full cooperation. I will keep your confidence."

"It will require a lot of manpower. I suggest we start with hospital emergency rooms and clinics. Check for anyone with a bullet in his shoulder. The wounded guy will seek medical care. Stake out these facilities and the usual criminal haunts. Alert our informants. Tell 'em there's a handsome reward. They'll bust their butts."

Serge continued his instructions. "Search the entire Baja peninsula for a beat-up VW combi van with a shattered rear window. Sorry. Don't have a license number for you."

"Got it, Serge. Our entire barracks will be out in full force. No weekend off for anyone, we'll be all over this case."

Serge and Biff were pleased at the sergeant's sudden change in attitude. They had his full cooperation.

Perhaps Serge's whispered reminder that he'd arranged a job three years ago for Roberto's son played a role in the sergeant's mood swing.

The favor returned, the score was now even.

Graciously, Roberto shook Biff's hand, almost apologetically, "No más preguntas, Señor. Buena suerte con su hijo perdido." (No more questions, sir. Good luck with your lost boy.")

"Gracias, Roberto." Biff grinned at Serge, who softly sighed with relief.

What Biff didn't know was just how close he came to involving the Federales in this case. Not dealing with them was paramount. They could fuck up a Sunday school picnic!

CHAPTER FIVE
THE RECAP NOON SATURDAY

After wrapping up the details with the local police and delegating responsibilities, Biff and Serge adjourned to the Roberts' suite to recap the morning's astonishing events. They required a sound "game plan" to address this heinous crime interfering with their mission.

As they walked back, Serge observed Biff's demeanor, reflecting on his distinguished career. He'd known him for years, marveled at his career achievements.

"Here's a guy who going through Hell and high water, up to his ass in alligators, and he still has it all together. Still looks quite fit. Must be pushing sixty. How's he do it?"

Serge was awed by Biff's legendary command. He'd just witnessed a command performance, representing one of many hallmark characteristics that propelled Biff to the highest rank among CIA field officers dealing in National intelligence, security, and international clandestine affairs.

Some at Langley predicted that after retirement, this man would be mentioned in the same breath as the legendary CIA operatives, Lansdale and Conien. That would not surprise Serge, not one bit. Biff was a major player in the company.

"Buford Cavendish Roberts V", he mused. A remarkable man of talent and achievement - The Vietnam conflict, Central America during the Sandanista- Contra conflict, name it, and Biff was involved big time."

"Shhhh…my wife may be sleeping." Biff warned as he quietly unlocked their suite's door.

"The considerate manager brought her some Ambien to sedate her. I understand it doesn't require a prescription down here. She's on the verge of a nervous breakdown, Serge."

"Smart move! I can understand her needing a sedative, Biff. This is extremely stressful for both of you. You are highly trained, conditioned to face adversity. She's not. She's a mother whose son has been abducted. Naturally, she fears the worse. Personally, I'd keep her sedated for awhile, until she can get a grip on this devastating situation with our support."

"You have a good point, Serge."

"Assure her that we will find Boo. The Baja peninsula is compact. Not a lot of places to hide an American 14 year old. I promise you, pal. I've got contacts up the kazoo. A lot of chips out there. I plan to call 'em in."

"I appreciate your help Serge", Biff said as he quietly slipped the key from the Suite's door lock.

As they entered Biff noted the bedroom door was shut. Mary Beth was 'out like a light', otherwise she would have greeted him as usual.

"It's OK. She's sleeping. Let's talk quietly over here, Serge. Let me get something cold to drink for us."

The two veteran field officers sat in the comfortable rattan sofas in Biff's spacious, fancy suite, sipping OJ with a shot of vodka, "screwdrivers".

"Ahh… refreshing", Biff commented. "The orange juice down here is so fresh. They squeeze it with every order"

"Sure hits the spot. Good choice. Guess you can use a drink after the morning you've experienced, Biff. Unfucking real, man!"

Serge glanced out the suite's window. His two bodyguards had stationed themselves on the balcony, ever vigilant while the two CIA field officers conferred inside.

"So, what now, Serge? I came down here to consult with you on Sandoval's drug cartel's gunrunning ambitions, and before we even get started, those Mexican bastards snatch our son! Talk about a RF!"

"It's unreal! I cannot recall one instance like this involving a kidnapping. Cabo is an international trade free zone, a hot tourist spot. Mexico's goal is to maintain Baja's 'jewel' as tranquil as San Diego. The Government wants to keep those American dollars flowing in steadily. The Federales enforce tight security."

"So now, Biff, I figure we've got two missions. The original one, involving interdiction of Sandoval's cartel ambitions, and a new one, recovering your son, ASAP. Boo is our top priority, I assure you."

"Your plan, Serge?"

"I'll get the recovery operation rolling right away. As I mentioned, Biff, I've got a lot of contacts after 30 years down here. I'll get the word out right away. We're on a peninsula that has limited road access. We have a few small towns, lots of resorts, but the rest is desert and mountains. The inhospitable Baja terrain is easy to survey by plane or choppers. We'll be all over it."

"As we discussed outside moments ago with the local police, we'll stake out the medical facilities. Not many of those. Don't see a lot of gunshot wounds down here, so the guy you nailed in the shoulder will be reported to us by the medical staff when he seeks treatment. That is, if he shows up and manages to slip through our surveillance teams outside the facility. We'll snare him!"

"Kidnapping is a huge transgression in our Mexican culture, especially if it involves children. These Latinos are big on families, strong ties and loyalties. They are good people. Mexicans put up with a lot of petty crimes, but draw the line when anybody messes with kids. Kidnapping is contemptible, universally condemned down here. It's considered an egregious crime. They throw the book at the apprehended culprits."

"I assure you the public will be alerted and be on the lookout for Boo. They will cooperate and report any suspicious activity. Finding your boy is our top priority, Biff, we'll address the cartel business in due order."

Serge arose to depart. Biff jumped up to thank him.

"Thanks pal", shaking Serge's hand, patting him on his back with the other in a collegial fashion.

"Sure grateful for all your help", Biff escorted him to the door.

The sea breeze caught the door, slamming it just as Serge departed.

He peeked back in the doorway to apologize.

"Sorry, Biff. The wind got it. Later, hombre," as he eased the door shut this time.

The noise of the slamming door awakened Mary Beth. She rushed out of the bedroom, alarmed. Her nerves were frazzled, worried that Biff may be involved in another "shoot out".

"Biff, what was that loud bang?"

"The wind inadvertently slammed the door, as Serge left. Sorry, dear."

"The noise scared me. I'm a bit on edge, Biff."

"I understand, Dear."

"Oh, did you two work out something regarding Boo?"

"We've got a game plan in motion, honey. We're going to get Boo back. I promise you. Serge has an operation mounted. He's very resourceful."

He went over and gave her a big hug and a kiss.

"Oh no!", she exclaimed.

"What's up?" Her sudden response surprised him.

"I forgot to notify Caroline about Boo. I better call now."

"There's only one hour's difference in time between here and in Arizona. She should be up by now. Give her a call, dear."

Biff had spaced it also. He was remiss in not letting their daughter know earlier about her brother's abduction.

Almost magically, her call went through right away. The first thing that had gone right all day.

"Caroline, this is Mom. You are not going to believe this, but your brother, Boo, has been kidnapped! Just a short while ago."

"What?! No way, Mom…"

As his bodyguards drove him back to the consulate, Serge empathized with Biff. "Most guys would have folded. Gone into a 'bunker mentality' under this pressure."

Serge commiserated with Biff's wife. She was an emotional wreck.

"Next to death, kidnapping grips the maximum stress threshold and never lets go until the problem is resolved", Serge introspected.

"Poor lady is beside herself, searching for answers."

"But, Biff just keeps plugging along. I know it's killing him inside, but he's the living definition of resilience. He's one tough hombre!"

Serge reflected on his own fractured family life. It was sorrowful. Maybe there was a life lesson here. Communication represented the keystone to reconciliation.

"WTF! I'm gonna contact my kids and start over, as soon as I can, if I can ever figure out where the Hell they are! Might have to call in the FBI!"

CHAPTER SIX

SANTIAGO NAVAL BASE, CUBA - SATURDAY

"**S**í, Comandante", the Lt. politely replied to the phone caller's question.

His boss personified the classic 'control freak'. He had learned to live with it. Those who did not were no longer in the Cuban Naval Command. His job demanded that he 'kiss ass', if he ever hoped to be promoted.

"The submarine is presently submerged in 40 fathoms, 20 kilometers off the coast of our first rendezvous point."

"Sí, your memory is correct. The sub passed through the Panama Canal last year without incident. You recall it was an old Soviet diesel, not a nuclear sub. No one viewed it as a threat. The Canal authorities bought the story that the sub was headed to the Marine Museum on the west coast of Mexico, to be on exhibit in the deep water port of Manzanillo."

"Yes, Sir, they waved it through after a brief inspection. Not a ripple of suspicion. All the paper work is in order. The sub is awaiting a scheduled annual sea trial this week. Planned departure is in the next twenty four hours."

"Sí, Comandante, the 'special' shipment arrived in Veracruz last week. It is being transported by truck across Mexico…Sí…The canisters are carefully covered by bales of hay, Comandante."

"Sí, we have taken all the proper precautions. The special shipment is hermetically sealed in industrial strength, heavy duty plastic, and placed in three stainless steel, waterproof canisters…Sí…Labeled 'PELIGROSA!' (dangerous)."

"Sí, Comandante. No one will dare tamper with them. Sí, they will arrive on time according to our schedule, Comandante."

"Sí, our Mexican conspirators are in the loop, Comandante…Sí…Sí…I have 'double checked' every detail. I guarantee they will arrive on time in Manzanillo. No problema!"

"OK, Comandante, I will triple check all the details again, immediately. Yes sir!"

Comandante Rudolfo Blanco left nothing to chance. He had waited a lifetime for the approaching culmination of his career, "Operation Cabo Caper."

CHAPTER SEVEN
CABO CONSULATE –
SATURDAY AFTERNOON

"Thanks for sending a driver, Serge."

"No problem. By the way, Henre's more than just a driver. He's an expert in martial arts, and a sharpshooter. I've assigned him to you for the remainder of your stay. We'll also assign someone to look out for your wife."

"Thanks! That works for me, Serge."

"How's it going?"

"It was a tough morning, pal. Mary Beth is still struggling with our ordeal. At least she got some sleep with the medication."

"Good. That's a positive."

"Any leads on our boy, Serge?"

"Not yet. Got the ball rolling, but you know it's a process. Hang in there."

"I'm trying, pal. It's more than a major distraction. It's tough for me to deal with. I can't imagine how painful and difficult it is for my wife!"

Biff abruptly switched topics.

"OK, my good man. Brief me on my original mission. Let's get down to business. I need to deal with another subject."

"Sure, Biff. I understand."

"Here's the story in a nutshell. Ricardo Sandoval leads a well organized cartel, very successful in smuggling pot and coke into the States. Very elusive character, always a step ahead of the authorities. Just when we think we're about to nab him, he slips away. Ricardo is a fucking Houdini!"

"We think his gang is presently operating out of the Baja peninsula, after the Federales' heat became too intense up along the border. Also, the cartel turf rivalries became violent up there recently. The combination of those two factors motivated Sandoval to abandon his lucrative setup up north. The man is remarkably innovative, independent, and flexible. He adapts to the dynamic trafficking patterns adroitly."

"Once it became obvious that the status quo up on the border was no longer tenable, he made his move. Sandoval is not one to go with the flow. Not one to truce or compromise. He chose to relocate his cartel."

"As cartels go, Sandoval's is relatively non- violent. Not a 'shoot 'em up' type of gang. They will take defensive action, but not aggressively go after another cartel's turf. That makes them an exception to the rule."

"Sandoval saw this chaotic situation, however, as a business opportunity. He's a clever dude. He's come up with a scheme to make big profits coming and going. Ricardo decided to 'feed the beast.' "

"How's that, Serge?"

"He takes the illicit drug money profits obtained in the U.S. and arranges for straw men to buy automatic assault rifles, ammo, and handguns at gun shows and from legitimate dealers. He then smuggles the weapons and ammo back across the border through the porous borders of the Southwest deserts."

"The cartels favor AK- 47's. Sandoval imports them by the dozens. No problem selling them for a considerable profit. That's a big time semiautomatic weapon, Biff. Lethal. The cartels now outgun the police. Little wonder the violence is escalating. Mexico's calling in the Army to deal with a situation bordering on anarchy.

"There is another consideration involving basic economics in these transactions. Simple 'supply and demand,' Biff."

"Big market for gunrunners in Mexico. These crazy fuckers are armed to the teeth, like small armies! Fortunately, they're mostly intent on killing each other in turf wars. Unfortunately, many innocent civilians are collateral damage in the wild shootouts."

"That is worse than 'unfortunate', it's outrageous, Serge."

"You got that right!"

"So, Ricardo's developed a clever plan, 'sell drugs, buy guns, sell guns'. I suspect Sandoval is doubling his money with this new twist in trafficking," Biff interjected.

"More like tripling his profits! Bought any ammo lately? These cartels shoot it up in gang fights like Rambo on steroids! They run though a lot of bullets, let me tell you, Biff. These trigger-happy bastards will empty their clips on a rival gang before you can blink an eye, then reload and keep on firing. They are absolutely nuts!"

"Sounds like a strong indication to bring down their operation before it escalates, Serge".

"It's already escalating, Biff. That's one reason we invited you down here to consult. Gangs like Ricardo's are creating chaos throughout Mexico, Central and South America. It won't be long before the violence spills across the border into the States. Then you're talking a major 'drug war'. That's a nightmare scenario!"

"The situation is much more serious than I realized, Serge. You know, I recall this Sandoval character from a takedown with the DEA in San Francisco in the late '60's, when we busted Rajah's 'Burma Gold' cartel. Ricardo Sandoval got away that time too. You're right, he's an elusive S.O.B.'"

"Sinister looking guy with a permanent sneer and a pencil thin mustache, I recall, Serge.'

"That's him. His sneer resulted as a complication of 'Bell's Palsy', as a kid."

"We've got to bring him down, Biff."

"Do you have a plan?"

"I do, my good man. Let me run it by you. I figure with our combined years of experience, we should be able to pull it off. I'm very interested in your input."

"OK, Serge, roll it …"

CHAPTER EIGHT

CABO SURF RESORT – ROBERTS' SUITE – LATER SATURDAY PM

Biff had just returned from his briefing with Serge at the consulate. His driver said he'd keep an eye out for any suspicious activity on the premises while Biff spent some time in his suite. Biff noticed the other guard on their balcony watching him, alert to any potential danger.

Biff needed to sit down and think things through. He greeted the guard and gently opened the door.

His wife was still sleeping. The considerate manager had given her a bottle of Ambien, no prescription necessary in Mexico. One pill did the trick. Mary Beth was stressed out. She needed some rest. The manager seemed sincerely tuned in to their stressful circumstances.

"Serge recommended the correct approach. Best to keep her sedated until she regains enough emotional control to deal with the trauma of Boo's abduction," Biff thought to himself, as he approached the bar across their suite's living room.

Biff poured himself a gin and tonic, settled into a comfortable chair, and started running through the various problems confronting him.

Just as he considered the most logical scenarios and sequences, the doorbell rang interrupting his train of thought.

"Jesus Christ! Give me a break!" an unusual outbreak of irritation for him. Self control under pressure usually characterized his personality.

He ran to the door, hoping to avoid a second ring awakening his wife. It was the manager, again.

"This fellow is up here every five minutes, it seems," he thought.

"Sorry to bother you again, but I wanted to report a couple of positive developments."

Biff's guard turned, and moved a few steps away, not wanting to intrude on a private conversation.

"My brother-in-law is the mayor of Cabo San Lucas. I apprised him of your tragic circumstances, facing a family crisis shortly after your arrival. He was astonished that your son was abducted. Said it was unprecedented. He is flying in two kidnap experts from Mexico City tonight to assist in the investigation. Also, he has spoken personally to the Cabo chief of police and the local commander of the Federales to insure a maximum effort is exerted, even though it is a weekend."

"Thank you very much, Señor, err..."

"Delarosa, Andres", he handed Biff his embossed business card.

"It is the least I could do in this regretful situation. Our security fell down on the job while changing shifts. We will remedy that, but it is too late now. We are so sorry that this happened."

His voice rang with sincerity. Biff contemplated that this resort represented Andres' life. He was proud of its reputation and he did not want to lose it. This was his 'child,' in essence.

"Will you and your wife be our guests this evening for dinner?"

"Thank you, but my wife simply will not be up to it. She is too distressed. By the way, thanks for the sedative."

"You are welcome. In that case, I insist we treat you to room service."

Biff thought a moment. They'd not had a meal since their arrival, being so preoccupied with their ordeal.

"That works fine for me, thank you."

"Any preferences?"

"Fresh fish, nice white wine..."

"Our chef will prepare Dorado caught this afternoon. I suggest a nice French Chablis from our select cellar."

"That will suit us fine, Andres. Thank you for your consideration."

The manager was laying it on, trying to make some small amends. It was quite obvious he was upset about the stunning kidnapping occurrence this morning. It turned the resort upside down. No one had stopped talking about it.

"Time?"

"About 8 pm."

"You will not be disappointed, Señor Roberts."

Mary Beth awoke around 7 pm, rested, a bit more in control of her emotions. She resigned to be more supportive of Biff in this tragic situation. He plugged ahead under all circumstances. She needed to step up. Stand by him.

"Oh, you're awake, dear. You needed the rest. It's been a traumatic day. We've got a lot going. We will find Boo", he tried to appear up beat. Keep his wife's sprits up.

She marveled at his resiliency. His optimism. They'd been married 30 years and she still did not understand what drove him. How he always faced adversity head on. As if nothing fazed him. No challenge too big.

"How do you manage to handle this crisis so well, Biff? You act like you are in command. We are in a foreign country facing a tragedy. How do you propose to rescue Boo?"

"Serge and I are working on that. We have a lot of irons in the fire. I have every confidence we will recover our son, dear."

"How do you know?", she challenged him'

"I just do. 'He said with affirmation." Believe me, dear."

"I don't understand you, Biff."

"You can't control the world or change it. But, you can control your reaction to it. You can fold up your tent and let life's events run over you, or you can stand up to the challenges and conquer them. I intend to do just that, my dear. I promise you that we will find Boo and bring him home. I know how upset you are, but you just have to trust me on this, OK?"

"Serge's got a lot of contacts. Cabo is a small area. We'll find him. We'll push through this. Hang in there!"

It was a rare moment of introspection. After all these years she had a glimpse of Biff's inner soul.

What made him remarkable?

What made him tick?

What made her love him?

Biff suddenly changed the topic.

"Better dress up, honey."

"Why in Heaven's sake should I dress up? I have no intention of going out." His request out of the blue surprised her.

"The manager is treating us to room service at 8 pm."

"How nice of him. Actually, I am hungry, Biff. We haven't had a bite since we arrived. How considerate."

"He feels bad about what happened this morning, dear, and is trying to show his concern. He strikes me as sincere in his efforts. He's enlisted some high power assistance from the local authorities. Told me his brother–in-law is the mayor of Cabo, who is flying in two kidnap experts from Mexico City tonight."

"Really?"

Her tone sounded uplifted by this news, as he hoped it would. She needed his positive input.

They enjoyed the dinner. The manager did not exaggerate. The meal and presentation were San Francisco caliber. The wine soothed them. They almost found themselves relaxed for a moment. They spoke little, since the topic of Boo was too painful to voice. They needed a short respite from that preoccupation and conversation.

But, Boo never really left their thoughts. The emotional impact of their loss still riveted their minds, defying expression. Flashbacks of the ugly episode recurred uninvited, intruding on their consciousness, pounding their emotional reserve without pity with its stark, brutal reality. Boo was gone! The enormity of their tragedy was still sinking in relentlessly, like an obsession.

As soon as the waiter cleared the table, they went directly to bed, both exhausted and strung out from the day's stress. The disheartened couple tossed and turned for an hour before finally falling asleep.

Restless, Mary Beth reflected on Biff's remarks. Most people she knew followed the herd, conformed. A few marched to their own drummer. But, in her husband's case, he marched to his own band.

Before she drifted off, she thought about their long relationship. Her thoughts flashed back to their early relationship, over 40 years ago, before they were married. In college, they dated for four wonderful years. While at Yale, Biff was recruited by the CIA and later became a career CIA field officer. He spent the next six years posted to the U.S. Embassy in Saigon under diplomatic cover. Even though he couldn't discuss his work, Mary Beth knew that Biff conducted dangerous top secret, clandestine missions in Vietnam. She never knew if or when he would return to San Francisco to marry her as he promised.

She waited faithfully six years for him, worrying constantly about his safety. As promised, he returned from Vietnam just before the infamous January 1968 Tet attacks.

They soon married, but unfortunately they spent little time together since Biff was always off somewhere in some foreign country for extended periods, thwarting Communism and insurrection. It was tough at times not hearing from him, wondering if he was still alive.

She persevered, raised their two children, always waiting anxiously for his brief returns to live a "normal" life together as a family.

Now that Biff had attained a high ranking consultant position with the Company, their life was finally returning to reasonable normalcy. That is, until this morning when Boo was kidnapped. Their family vacation suddenly turned into a catastrophe!

Now their life had been turned upside down.

"Oh my God! Will Biff be able to rescue him?"

She thought long and hard. He's always come through before, often against all odds. Why not now? The higher the stakes, the more remarkable his performance. Her spirits lifted.

"Yes, Biff was exceptional."

She smiled with that thought in mind, and fell asleep.

A couple of hours later the doorbell rang, Biff climbed out of bed, checked his watch. It was12.30 am. He instinctively grabbed his Beretta, forgetting there was a guard posted outside on his balcony.

"Who is it?" he enquired though the door.

"Andres, the manager. Sorry to bother you at this hour, but, it is urgent." His inflection was convincing.

"Not again", Biff muttered placed his gun on the table next to the door and opened the door.

His guard kept an eye on the manager. No one was above suspicion, Serge's orders.

"What's up, Andres?"

"Sorry to bother you at this hour, but a delivery boy on his bike insisted that it was very important, that I should give this letter to you immediately."

He handed Biff a fancy envelope that looked like a fancy invitation of some sort.

Biff rubbed his eye. It was still irritated from this morning's shaving cream mishap. He was groggy.

"Thank you, Andres."

As the resort manager departed, he thought, "Poor guy. One thing after another…"

Biff bid the sentry 'Good night' for the second time.

Buenas noches", he replied.

Biff went to a far corner of the room, turned on a light and put on his reading glasses.

"That's puzzling. I've been here less than 24 hours and I'm receiving special delivery mail in the middle of the night? Serge agreed to communicate by coded E-mail only. This letter is addressed with my formal name. Only Serge knows that detail down here. Something is wrong with this picture!"

Biff felt anxious, threatened by a series of unexpected and unexplained occurrences, challenging his resolve. His wife was putting on a brave face, but her status appeared fragile. Clearly, it was up to him and Serge to pull this off.

He could feel his pulse racing as he carefully examined the letter, fearing what message it may convey inside. The letter's looked and felt like parchment.

"Pretty fancy paper", he mused.

The typed font was distinctly unusual, somewhere between italics and calligraphy, or maybe a combination of the two. Biff did not recognize the font. Another enigma!

MR. B. C. ROBERTS V
SUITE 20
CABO BEACH RESORT

Biff opened the envelope and read its message. The communication was not cryptic. It was shockingly blunt!

MR. ROBERTS,

REST ASSURED THAT YOUR SON IS SAFE AND UNHARMED. HE WILL BE RETURNED TO YOU ONE WEEK FROM TODAY IF YOU COMPLY WITH OUR TERMS:

ONE – ONE MILLION US DOLLARS RANSOM TO BE WIRED TO A NUMBERED ACCOUNT IN THE CAYMAN ISLANDS. YOU WILL NOT RECEIVE THE ACCOUNT WIRING INSTRUCTIONS UNTIL NEXT SATURDAY AT THE LAST MINUTE TO PREVENT TRACING THE NUMBER.

TWO – YOU HAVE ONE WEEK TO COMPLY. ONCE THE FUNDS ARE RECEIVED AND VERIFIED OUR ACCOUNT WILL BE CLOSED. IT IS SET UP UNDER AN ASSUMED NAME. YOU CANNOT TRACE IT, EVEN IF YOU HAD TIME.

THREE – ONCE THE RANSOM IS RECEIVED, YOUR SON WILL BE RELEASED UNHARMED. WE WILL NOTIFY YOU OF THE RELEASE LOCATION FIVE MINUTES BEFORE WE DROP HIM OFF, DEPRIVING YOU OF THE OPPORTUNITY TO STAKE OUT OUR POSITION. SO, DO NOT EVEN TRY!

FOUR – BOO IS A FINE BOY. FOLLOW OUR INSTRUCTIONS CAREFULLY IF YOU WISH TO SEE HIM AGAIN.

FIVE – IF THESE TERMS ARE AGREEABLE, LEAVE A RED BEACH TOWEL HANGING OVER YOUR BALCONY RAIL TONIGHT. NO TOWEL, NO DEAL!

Beads of sweat covered Biff's forehead. He clinched his teeth, raging with anger.

"Those miserable bastards! They thought it all out. It's virtually impossible to trap them!" he muttered to himself.

After rereading the ransom note twice, he contacted Serge on an emergency 24/7 secure line.

"You gotta see the ransom note I just received…"

Before Biff could finish his sentence Serge broke in, "Hold on. I'll be right over!"

Biff quietly retrieved a large red beach towel, went to the balcony and carefully hung it over the rail, so it could not blow away. It was now 1 am Sunday morning.

The sentry looked puzzled by Biff's action at this hour, but, respectably, said not a word.

Biff glanced at him, and sensed his curiosity.

"Don't move it! It's a signal, comprende?"

"Si, Señor." He replied, more confused than ever.

Before returning to bed, Biff sat in the dimly lit living room, contemplating his dilemma. He'd been in difficult predicaments before, but he never had been confronted with a problem of this magnitude, especially one with a very personal twist.

His thoughts flashed back to his Vietnam experience, over forty years ago. He recalled an oft quoted witticism from those tumultuous days.

"When you are up to your ass in alligators, it's hard to remember your objective was to drain the swamp!"

CHAPTER NINE

TODOS SANTOS, MEXICO –
LATE SATURDAY EVENING

"**T**he boy alright?"

"Si, Ricardo. Padre Miguel says he ate all his dinner and is resting comfortably at the church. The nuns will keep a close eye on him. He's responding to their loving attention. The boy is confused. He didn't expect considerate treatment, especially reassuring hugs from the nuns. We posted a guard outside in the hallway out of his sight. Don't want to scare him. I doubt he'll try to escape."

It was approaching midnight in this quiet colonial town near the tip of Baja about 70 miles from Cabo. The rural town did not attract many tourists, except 'Eagles' aficionados familiar with their hit tune 'Hotel California' with its famous lyrics, 'you can check out, but never leave…"

These cult fans would drive over the narrow mountain road at their peril for lunch, a beer, and a curiosity tour.

The hotel lacked the glamour and excitement of Cabo, rather ordinary and humble in appearance and amenities. After lunch, the visitors would stand in line by the commemorative plaque for a photo op to show the folks back home that they visited this spiritual spot. Then they hustled back to Cabo before dark. No one wanted to deal with that dangerous road at night.

Consequently, you could figuratively roll up the town's main road at dusk. Only a few locals ventured out at night, then usually only on Friday and Saturday nights. They couldn't afford to go out more often. They were poor by American standards. Besides, their choices were limited to church or the Hotel California activities.

Tonight a few local stragglers remained at the hotel's bar, well into their cups, "baracho", watching a late replay of a football game between Mexico City and top rival Guadalajara. The TV was an old black and white box that flickered on and off when the wind gusted, blowing the aerial on the roof, a frequent occurrence by the Pacific coast of Baja. Westerly gusts often reached 20 to 30 knots. The TV aerial bent like a twig in the high winds.

As a result, the game progressed with many interruptions, frustrating the drunken viewers, who were practically falling off their barstools as the night wore on. Not much else to do on Saturday night. No night clubs, dance halls, or whore houses. This was the only game in town. Their idea of whooping it up.

"Jose, why don't you fix the damn TV?", one fan complained for the tenth time." Can't keep track of the fucking game!"

The bartender ignored him for the tenth time. He was tired and wanted to go home. No chance. It was only half time. He'd endure another hour or so of their drunken gibes and revelry.

Huddled in an adjacent private room, a sinister game was being played. The room's dark, moldy atmosphere seemed appropriate for these men who lived on the dark side of life.

Jorge Gomez was in the process of updating his boss on Boo Roberts' condition. Jorge was a short, stout man in his mid–fifties, balding with sparse gray hair. He routinely dressed in elegant, expensive earth toned guyabaras, a traditional Mexican wedding shirt, customarily worn without a tie, shirt tail out. The shirt nicely hid his rotund abdomen, probably why he chose to wear them on most occasions over tailored linen trousers. Jorge sported around Cabo in this fancy attire attracting only casual notice, but in provincial Todos Santos his attire was definitely was over the top. He stood out like a Ferrari in a one horse town in this outfit, attracting curious glances, turning heads, and even a few rude comments.

Jorge presented a classy, aristocratic Latino appearance as he briefed Ricardo Sandoval and cartel members around the candle lit table. In stark contrast, they wore more traditional duds, Levi's, cowboy shirts, and boots.

The chandelier's bulbs that burnt out months ago had not been replaced. The table candles flickered in the drafty, dark room. The remains of their dinner and the dirty dishes had not been cleared by the waiter who doubled as the village idiot. An assortment of empty wine bottles, some of expensive French origin, littered the ancient wooden rector's table. The room's furnishings were dated, worn, and dusty. The room reeked of tobacco. The ashtrays hadn't been emptied in days, if not a week. The noise and smoke from the bar filtered into their "private" room. Not an elegant setting, but they sought seclusion, not ambience.

"Disgusting!" Jorge thought. He wished they could meet elsewhere, but no alternative existed in this "one horse" town, with only one sign greeting, 'Welcome. Come Again', he joked.

But, he reconsidered, this place is off the beaten path, safe. That's why Ricardo Sandoval elected to hide out in Todos Santos. No one would look for them here.

Jorge resumed his briefing in perfect Spanish with a Castilian accent flare, disdaining slang or Mexican inflection. He preferred sophistication in his speech and presentation.

This pissed off most of the cartel who considered him haughty, and pretentious. But everyone respected his intelligence. Jorge kept the books and was the paymaster, never cheating anyone.

Ricardo Sandoval viewed him as pseudo-sophisticated, but a valuable associate whom he could trust to keep the books and manage the financial aspects of their lucrative drug and recently emerging weapon trafficking business. Jorge was a "numbers" man he could rely on. So, he tolerated Jorge's peccadilloes. Ricardo chose a pragmatic approach in business and in life.

Jorge resumed his briefing to the gnarly group.

"Padre Miguel assures me that he and the nuns will carefully care for the boy, who seems to trust them already. He appears to be a tough little youngster. No crying or whining."

"Ricardo, are you certain that we can trust the Padre not to inform anyone of his whereabouts, or let the boy escape?"

"Miguel is my younger brother, Jorge. Remember?"

He rebuked his trusted Lieutenant.

"I've taken good financial care of him, regularly paid for his vacations in La Jolla. Last year I bought him a comfy little condo there. He owes me."

"But, how does the good Padre deal with the moral issue?"

"I've told Miguel that the boy's American father is an abusive alcoholic, becoming more violent by the day. I feared for the child's safety, so I took the boy away until we could straighten out the unfortunate family situation. I told him we're trying to get the father into a detox program, all in the youngster's best interests."

"What did he say to that, Ricardo? Sounds quite plausible."

"Miguel accepted my deceptive story, but objected to my process, essentially, 'kidnapping" the boy. He said that was 'wrong', a 'sin'."

"I appealed to his sense of moral relativity. That it was a worse 'sin' to expose the child to potential physical and emotional harm. I explained that I intended to use the boy as leverage to force his father to seek medical treatment. This was my last option to manage the father's egregious, abusive behavior."

"Did the Padre accept your reasoned explanation?"

"Only after I promised to come to confessional, say my rosary, and twelve Hail Mary's."

A chorus of laughter and guffaws erupted around the table from the cartel, an unruly lot. Sacrilegious, in fact.

Ricardo smiled at their mirth, Jorge just shook his head.

Jorge was amazed at Ricardo's guile. He was a cunning devil.

Probably, he would deceive his own mother!

"My brother does not understand that the boy is merely a pawn in our game with this Roberts fellow. I absolutely have no intention of harming the child."

A certain honor existed among thieves.

"I merely intend to screw with Roberts' mind, intimidate him, confuse and mislead him, keep him preoccupied searching for his son while we carry out our important mission."

"I'm not in the kidnapping business. Snatching his son was merely an expedient to create a distraction, Jorge. Let me tell you a little about this American CIA guy. You don't want to mess with him. He's one clever fox and he's in Cabo for one purpose and one purpose only, to bring us down!"

"I haven't forgotten what he did to Rajah's cartel in San Francisco back in '69. I was lucky to escape with my life! I'll never forget the awesome shootout in the Mission district!"

"We've got to be very careful. I don't want Roberts to fuck up our deal with the Cubans. Do not underestimate his resourcefulness. Take every precaution and stick to our game plan, OK? No slip ups. It'll be your last!"

"If we pull this deal off, it will make our drug and gun trafficking operation profits look like peso pocket change!"

That statement caught the cartels' full attention. They sat up and leaned forward, "Yeah, man!"

They hadn't the slightest notion what the Cuban mission was, or what it entailed. All they heard was that 'big money' was involved. That turned them on.

"We cannot afford to let this Gringo mess with our plans. I've spent a year organizing this Cabo caper down to the smallest detail."

"How did you know this Roberts fellow was in Cabo, Ricardo?"

Jorge was smart and inquisitive. This question would never have occurred to the others, Ricardo reflected.

"I've got my sources. Very reliable sources," he sneered and laughed heartedly.

Their boss's cleverness impressed his cartel. His shrewdness never ceased to amaze them. Surely that accounted for the fact that they eluded the authorities time after time.

Ricardo was not an imposing figure, but distinctively unforgettable. Once you saw him, his unusual appearance became etched in your mind.

A tall, thin Hispanic with jet black hair combed straight back. Hairspray prevented a single hair dislodging even in the strong coastal breezes. The left side of his lip curled up in a permanent sneer, the result of Bell's palsy. It gave him a sinister appearance to match his demeanor. Not one to mess with. No one dared. Ricardo personified evil.

His heavy gold necklace glistened, reflecting the candle light in the dark, dingy room. Ricardo wore a heavily starched shirt, open at the collar, revealing not only the necklace, but a generous amount of black hair on his suntanned chest. He manifested the 'macho look 'to the hilt. Ricardo perfected this 'look' with his carriage and demeanor.

His dark beady, piercing eyes completed his distinguishing features. He could look right though you, an unnerving experience.

The dark room reflected his mood. He was apprehensive that Biff Roberts might somehow contravene his well laid plans, despite the enormous distraction of dealing with his son's abduction. Ricardo did not fear Biff Roberts, but he respected him as a worthy adversary.

It made him quite anxious that Biff Roberts showed up in Mexico one week before their mission. He doubted that it was merely a coincidence. Timing of his special operation was critical, everything depended on it. A year's planning went into his commitment to the Cubans. He could not fail his mission.

Roberts's arrival probably wasn't coincidental, but how could his nemesis possibly know of their plan? Impossible!

"No way could the CIA know about it. No way… Could they?"

CHAPTER TEN

U.S. CONSULATE – CABO SAN LUCAS – EARLY SUNDAY AM

erge traveled from town in the middle of the night to Biff's suite, retrieved the ransom note, and after a short, reassuring conversation with Biff, he returned to his office around 1am Sunday.

He made several emergency calls to his forensic and detective staffs. Serge then placed another call to an unlisted number, the' contractors'.

He informed all of them that they should expect to be working steadily for the next 24 hours at least. A lot depended on their discoveries. He emphasized the stakes were high, a positive outcome imperative. He apologized for awakening them at this ungodly hour, but' get on the stick!' Swift action demanded this unusual request in the middle of the night.

They understood. The teams worked all night analyzing the ransom note for finger prints and DNA. They particularly focused on the parchment paper and the peculiar font type "Fascinating," they commented.

Teams were dispatched to the field with instructions to "leave no stone unturned.".

"Check every detail. No aspect too small. Consider this assignment as 'top priority,'" Serge urged them.

"Put yourself in my friend's place. How'd you like to trade places with him? Your child kidnapped?"

"That should motivate them to work all weekend without time off," he thought to himself.

Serge' prediction played out. Several important clues developed overnight. He was busily reviewing them when Alicia ushered in his good friend.

Biff showed up at Serge' office at 8 am sharp. He now had his own driver and bodyguard. Serge had assured him that he would not be stranded again on this trip.

Mary Beth had elected to take another Ambien in the middle of the night. Biff figured she'd still be sleeping for another 6 to 8 hours. Serge had assigned a bodyguard to her also. Her guard stationed himself on the suite's balcony, armed with a Colt .45.

Biff left her a considerate note regarding his plans, whereabouts, and intentions:

"Back around noon. Got a driver now. Off to meet Serge. Love, Biff," he signed off.

"Morning, Biff. Coffee?" Serge greeted him cheerfully.

"Obviously, he has some leads", Biff immediately assumed by the tone. He was pretty good at reading Serge's mood.

"Sure, Serge. Thanks. Maybe a donut?"

"Go one better. Alicia brought in a coffee cake."

The attractive Latina served them a generous portion of cake, poured them a large mug of espresso, politely smiled, and departed without a word.

She recognized that if the staff worked all night and planned to be on the job through the weekend that something big was coming down. She vicariously enjoyed the boy's exciting intrigues and games. She loved her job.

"Nice looking woman, Serge."

"Couldn't ask for a better secretary."

Despite being up all night, Serge was energized, animated. He had jumped full force into this case. A lot was riding on this case besides the kidnapping. They must not side tract their Sandoval mission. Complex, but a doable challenge.

Serge Betancourt hadn't been this pumped up in 20 years.

"OK, Biff. My team worked all night. Came up with some interesting clues."

"I'm all ears, shoot."

"First, the ransom note. Checked it for fingerprints. Found yours, the manager's, the desk clerk's, and we suspect the unknown prints are the delivery boy's, or the sender's. No criminal matches in our databases. Also, no DNA on the envelope. Obviously, they didn't lick the sealing glue. We sent samples to NSA at Langley to double check our results."

"My forensic experts were fascinated with the note's parchment paper and the unusual font. He Googled the font, It's 'Algerian'!"

"Algerian? What the Hell is that all about?" That revelation blew Biff away.

"My guy went a step further. His diligent research found that some Catholic churches used this particular font and parchment as far back as the late nineteenth century for special formal occasions, like weddings and christenings."

"I suspect the kidnappers used an old church typewriter with that peculiar font to type the ransom note. Forensics tells me that some old missions in Mexico and Central America still use these old typewriters on special occasions for formal missives."

Serge paused to let Biff ponder the implications of this discovery.

"All we have to do is check all the Catholic churches and missions on Baja. Elegant!" Biff elated, using a classic ivy league expression.

Serge didn't know whether to accept the 'elegant' comment as a compliment, or a code word for "BS". He chose not to question it, and pressed on.

"We're all over it, Biff. Checking all the churches in the vicinity for a match."

"Good man, Serge!"

"Secondly, consider the delivery boy," Serge continued. "Upon close questioning, the resort's night desk clerk told one of my agents that he thinks it's the same kid who works outside 'The Office 'on the beach in Cabo. Gave a good description. Kid hawks suntan lotion in the daytime, condoms at night. Very enterprising youngster, it seems."

"The Office?"… Biff enquired, puzzled. "Suntan lotion, condoms?"…

"It's a popular tourist hangout. Beachfront restaurant, large TV flat screens with good satellite reception from the States. Place catches all the games. Sport nuts flock there in droves. Food is not bad either. Inexpensive. Place is practically open 24/7 for beer and nachos. It's a fucking goldmine! Place is hopping day and night."

Serge' upbeat briefing relaxed Biff. He grinned and laughed. He appreciated Serge and his team staying up all night, coming up with valuable leads. He had spent a fitful night, tossing and turning.

"Really a good start, man!", he praised Serge, not showing his fatique.

"Anyways, Biff, we have our Mexican detectives hanging out at the 'office 'dressed like tourists, looking for the 'office boy'. If his prints match, we're off and running with an intense, focused interrogation. We don't have the restraints that encumber you in the States. We employ 'contractors', outsourcing, sorta like rendition. You know what I mean? We will find out who hired him and follow that lead."

Biff regretted that he knew what Serge 'meant'.

"OK, so that's where we stand on the abduction at this early stage. Now let's talk about our other mission. That's the reason you came down here, recall?"

Biff had almost lost sight of his original objective, immersed in his personal turmoil.

"I got the Director's memo. You filled in the gaps yesterday. Now I've got the big picture, Serge. Traffic drugs up to States, buy weapons and ammo with the profits, smuggle them back across the border and sell them to other cartels."

"You got it, Biff, except one important aspect that has international ramifications."

"How's that?"

"These fuckers peddle the firearms to insurgents in the Banana Republics in Central and South America, spreading chaos everywhere. That nutcase leader in Venezuela is a major buyer. These deals involve big time cash exchanges, serious money."

"If we can interdict Sandoval's operation, that'll put the others on notice that we are coming after them."

"I think I'm up to speed on our objectives, Serge."

"Biff, one other important thing… Some classified info came in over secure channels during the middle of the night. I happened to be here to pick it up. I'm sure you didn't receive it, or you would have mentioned it first thing upon your arrival this morning."

"What's that?"

"It's critical to our mission, Biff. The coded top-secret message I received from Langley links Sandoval somehow to Cuban terrorists!"

This pronouncement hit Biff like a brick. His jaw dropped. The mind-boggling news blew him away!

"How'd they come by that interesting tidbit of information? What's their source? Reliable? Their data?"

Biff believed in God, but everyone else had to show him their data.

"This is startling!", Biff exclaimed, stunned by this incredible news.

"NSA intercepts, Biff, and happenstance. NSA closely monitors all communications in and out of Cuba, electronic and otherwise. They've done so for decades, keeping a close eye on Fidel Castro and his boys. NSA postulates that Fidel is seeking a payback for the Bay of Pigs invasion way back in '61 and the ongoing crippling, decades long U.S. embargo of Cuba. He's been seething for years. He's getting old. May have cancer. Time's running out on him. If he's going to get even with us, he's got to make his move soon."

"So, what's Castro's plan? Did NSA say, Serge?"

"The recent intercept indicates that Castro intends to infiltrate terrorist hit men across our SW border into the U.S. through established drug cartel channels and routes, probably Arizona. The border is not secure there, no matter what Homeland Security asserts."

"What kind of terrorists? Any specifics?"

"No clue. Don't know what form they're plotting, Biff. The intercept indicated that the Cubans are shipping three steel containers to Mexico this month. What they contain remains a mystery. Don't know when or where. No details."

"Sandoval is in the loop in some way, probably as a facilitator, but his exact role is undisclosed at this point in time. A lot of loose ends right now, I'm sorry to say."

"Incredible scheme," Biff commented, shaking his head in wonderment.

"This really introduces a new, significant element into our mission, raising the stakes!"

"Got that right, Biff. We suspect they will ship the mystery containers up the Sea of Cortez to rendezvous with a trusted coyote to escort them across the Arizona or California border. NSA is dispatching one of their experts to closely monitor the developing situation from here."

"I guess they consider Cabo 'ground zero', Serge. Have you alerted the coast guard and appropriate authorities?"

"Step ahead of you. They've already started unannounced boardings and searches. It will bug the Hell out of the fishermen, but it will be a maximum effort. This is a BFD! Biff."

"You are right about that. Do you have an APB out on Sandoval? He has distinctive features, can't miss him."

"Yep, but remember you're in Mexico. Not everybody is wired in like in the States. It may take awhile. The forces are already mobilized, searching for your son. We'll just tack on this extra assignment. It will coincide with and intensify the effort. This is a bitch, man!"

Biff remained unusually quiet for a pause, pondering a theory, his mind churning on fast forward.

"Anything the matter, Biff?"

"You know, Serge, I've been thinking about something a little far out, but a plausible explanation for some of the unusual occurrences happening here. Maybe it ties in with the big picture."

"What's that?"

"Maybe Boo's kidnapping was not a random event. How'd they know I was in Cabo? Staying at the resort? Know my full name and suite number? My connection with you?"

"Serge, think about it. Maybe you have a paid informant, a 'mole' in your consulate. Just too many weird coincidences, in timing particularly, to explain otherwise. Someone is tipping off every move! Better check it out pronto, pal"

This declaration stunned Serge. The thought never occurred to him, but, if true, it explained a lot of things. Someone may be compromising their classified operations. Biff had zeroed in on a potentially critical flaw in the Consulate.

"A traitor in his inner circle? Unthinkable, but, if true, who could it possibly be?"

Serge did not have a clue!

"Good suggestion, Biff. Makes a lot of sense. I'll get right on it. Thanks!"

"Biff seems to have sixth sense. Remarkably sharp instincts.

"WTF! Why didn't I think of that?"

CHAPTER ELEVEN

HERNANDO'S HIDEAWAY — SAN JOSE MEXICO — 4 AM ON MONDAY

N o one would ever find him here. Everyone avoided the far NE edge of town where the poorest of the poor dwelled. The inhabitants did not really 'live 'here, they barely existed moment to moment, day to day. The ghetto consisted of shacks, shanties, and dilapidated cinder block buildings with cardboard sides, tin roofs, and broken windows. It was difficult to discern if the buildings were half constructed or destructed. In a word, the place was a 'mess.'

The ghetto defined 'grubby'. The most unfortunate endured despite the squalor of garbage and littered trash where feral cats fought stray dogs rummaging for a scrap of food. Rats thrived in this unsanitary environment. Chickens ran wild, scratching for a leftover or a dropping. It was a Darwinian jungle of sorts, including all inhabitants.

Flies and insects swarmed. Mosquitoes menaced everyone day and night in the hot and humid climate near the estuary of the Sea of Cortez. Some carried malaria, dengue, and encephalitis virus.

The 'dwellers' barely survived without electricity, running water, refrigeration, or sanitary amenities. They shared a community outhouse down by the creek where snakes thrived.

Not many took night trips down to the outhouse consequently.

Only the 'fittest' survived in this ramshackle environs.

It was an unusually hot and humid just before dawn in Hernando's dilapidated shack. He'd suffered through a second night of unrelenting agony.

"Hay mucho dolor!" he groaned and cried out in pain. Biff's bullet hit him from behind, lodging in his left shoulder, effectively enabling his left arm due to pain and swelling. The wound was hot, red, and draining malodorous serum, signs of infection. He experienced shaking chills during the night associated with a high fever. He felt like he was on fire. He couldn't think straight, at times delirious.

No Vicodin remained. He'd taken all of the analgesic, yet the pain remained unbearable. Almost 48 hours had passed since he was shot. He had to do something about his dilemma. He couldn't stand suffering another night. He was tapped out physically and emotionally spent.

The cartel strictly instructed him not to seek medical care, warning him that the authorities would stake out the facilities, looking for him. They gave him a bottle of pain pills, telling him to 'lay low'. They promised to arrange for a private surgeon to remove the bullet. That was two days ago, he hadn't heard from them. It was an empty promise. He couldn't bear the pain any longer.

Hernando glanced around his small room, looking for a bottle of water. He noted that he was down to his last two plastic containers. A dozen empty bottles littered the floor. His thirst seemed unquenchable.

He'd spent a second restless night, trying to find a comfortable position. He slept on a discarded dog bed on the dirt floor of his small, filthy one room shanty. He staggered to fetch the water, exhausted and weak. He gulped the warm water down. Only one bottle left to go with his last flour tortilla. After that he was out of provisions.

Hernando had spent his life in abject poverty. It didn't bother him that the door was falling off its hinges, the room's one window was broken, or that he ate off a wooden Tecate beer carton and sat on another. Nope, he could care less about these trivial considerations. He'd just made a bundle for his share of the compensation in the Cabo kidnapping caper. Enough to last a year. Enough to move out of this filthy place. Maybe get a real job and three square meals a day. He held optimism for his future for the first time in his 27 years, a unique experience.

If only he could manage to recover from his gunshot wound. That was his major concern at the moment.

Resigned that he must disobey Ricardo's lackeys' orders, Hernando struggled to get up to set out for the small medical dispensary about a mile or so away at the edge of town. It was about five am, he guessed, as dawn was breaking in the East over the sea. He put on his last clean jeans and an old white denim shirt. His other outfit was too bloodstained to wear. Even the simple act of dressing challenged him. He groaned and moaned, pulling the shirt over his injured shoulder.

He was unsteady in his feverish, weakened state. Usually a strong man, Hernando experienced a dizzy spell, bracing himself against the door frame to prevent falling. Regaining his balance, he stepped out into the feint light of early dawn, squinting to pick his pathway through the ghetto. He recognized that he had to reach medical care soon while he still possessed some strength and coherent thought, realizing his condition continued to deteriorate.

Suddenly, a mongrel dog chasing a cat scooted past him, almost knocking him over.

"Jesus Christo!", he swore.

The forty minute journey took its toll. It was grueling in his present condition. He stopped several times to rest and to catch his breath. He forced himself to press on, finally reaching his goal around quarter to six. The red sunrise on the horizon forecasted a hot day, as ground mist started to evaporate, increasing the humidity. Hernando was already soaked in sweat.

Even at this early hour, the dispensary was crowded with crying children accompanied by tired, worn out mothers. Old folks occupied the few remaining seats on the hard wooden benches, moaning from assorted ailments, some real, others imagined. A creaky ceiling fan circulated the stale, humid air. A mop and cleaning bucket stood by the entry, absent a janitor.

One of the youngsters vomited on the old terrazzo tiled floor of the waiting room creating a stench just as Hernando staggered into foyer, innervated by the mile journey from his hideaway.

He barely made his way to the reception desk, staggering, his shirt soaked with sweat, beads of perspiration running down his forehead to his cheeks. A wave of nausea swept over him. Thinking that he may pass out, he leaned against the sign- in desk, dizzy, too weak to speak, fighting a fear of falling to the floor. Somehow he regained his balance, prepared to announce the reason for his visit to the dispensary.

A beleaguered, experienced middle age R.N. looked up, assessing his condition. She was exhausted, up all night caring for the sick and disabled, but she immediately recognized this man was seriously ill and needed urgent medical attention.

"This man is hurting! Looks awful. Better get him into a treatment room right away so the Doctor can evaluate his condition." She was a veteran at triage after 20 years at the desk.

She noted the poor man couldn't move his left shoulder. Serum had seeped though the tattered, white cowboy shirt leaving a large putrid red stain. She smelled the distinctive odor of pus across her desk from three feet away. Obviously, the poor man was febrile from a wound infection. It looked like he was about to feint, steadying himself against her desk. She surmised he was septic and on the verge of going into shock, definitely an emergency.

Hernando finally mustered enough energy to speak.

"Tengo un problema grave!" I have a grave problem! He began.

Hernando got no further…

Two of Serge's agent 'contractors', moments earlier, observed Hernando stumbling into the dispensary, left arm dangling limply at his side. Taking shifts, their 'stakeout' was about to pay off.

This definitely was their man. The one they had waited almost 48 hours to nab.

Stealthily, they followed him to the receptionist's desk, closing in on their prey like predators.

"Got him!"

They grabbed Hernando roughly from behind, dragging him to the doorway, kicking and screaming in severe pain.

The astonished R.N. yelled, "Stop! What are you doing? That man is hurt!"

She was powerless, as were the onlookers in the waiting room. They sat quietly by, fearing a similar fate if they dared to intervene.

Once outside, they put a sack over his head and cruelly cuffed him.

Hernando cried out in excruciating pain, begging them to remove the handcuffs, explaining "It is killing my injured shoulder!"

Not a chance!

The agents harshly threw him in the back of their van and drove off to their 'safe-house' for an intense interrogation.

A rough ride ensued.

The Mexican CIA 'contractors' went right to work, strapping their captive in a heavy wooden chair in the middle of dank basement, padded with acoustic panels to dampen the victim's anguished cries.

Hernando slumped over in the chair, barely conscious, overwhelmed with pain and anxiety of what might happen next. He shook with fear in his helpless situation.

"Where the Hell did these mean hombres come from?"

"Who hired you to kidnap the boy? 'The elder contractor, Juan, demanded in a vicious, threatening tone.

No answer.

"O.K. Maybe this will help you to recall," he said menacingly.

Juan smiled at Enrique, took out a large Bowie hunting knife, and slit Hernando's shirt over his wounded shoulder.

Hernando's eyes widened, his pulse raced, his mouth dried so much that he could hardly express his fear, "Dear God!" he croaked…

Juan then heartlessly probed the captive's gunshot wound with the razor sharp point of the knife. Foul smelling pus spurted out under pressure, soiling Hernando's clothes and the concrete floor. The smell was rancid, permeating the small subterranean room with a rotten odor.

Hernando yelled in agony, turned pale, and passed out.

Enrique cringed at his partner's unbridled brutality. The putrid odor gagged him. The smell nauseated him. His partner's savage action repulsed him. He accepted the value of 'enhanced interrogation,' but Juan was pushing the envelope, torturing this kidnapper sadistically, crossing the line in his unbridled quest for critical information.

Juan sneered apathetically, threw a bucket of cold water in his face, and slapped Hernando across his face, commanding, "Now talk to me, hombre!"

Ironically, actually some of the excruciating pain in Hernando's shoulder was relieved by his tormentor's probing the wound. Draining the pus relieved a lot of pressure.

But, his shoulder still "hurt like Hell!"

Biff Roberts' bullet had shattered his scapula and lodged in his left shoulder joint. The shot barely missed the apex of his lung, major vessels and nerves.

Hernando was alive, but not well. Now he was being tortured by this crazed interrogator "What will this madman do next?" He shivered at the thought.

Juan had no sympathy for the abductor. He intended to teach him a lesson he'd never forget. Primitive punishment. No analgesia, no anesthesia, no mercy. Pure sadism.

Kidnapping was considered a heinous crime, especially in family oriented Mexico. The punishment should fit the crime. Juan intended to inflict maximum pain to extract the critical information he sought with unrelenting aggressiveness.

"Dígame! Tell me", he again commanded, twisting the sharp tip of the knife in Hernando's inflamed wound.

"No más! Por favor, no más", he pleaded with his captors, whimpering in distress. "No more, please," he begged.

He then vomited, gagging to avoid aspiration.

"Quien es su jefe? Como se llama? Dígame el nombre!", demanding the name of his boss.

"Dónde está él ahora?", where is he now?"

The knife probed again, deeply this time, eliciting a louder scream of anguish, followed by Hernando lapsing into another short period of unconsciousness. Clearly he was weakening by the minute.

"Maybe you should back off a bit, Juan. You're killing him!' '

Enrique felt uneasy with the severity of his partner's inexorable inquisition.

"I guarantee he'll talk," Juan replied sadistically.

No way would he back off. He threw another bucket of cold water in Hernando's face, slapped him again to arouse him. There would be no let up despite his partner's admonition.

"Dígame!" He brandished the Bowie knife in his face, and banged the steel handle hard against Hernando's wounded shoulder.

The captive screamed in aggravated pain, sobbed, and begged once more for mercy.

Juan slapped him across his face viciously, "Dígame!" "Tell me!"

Hernando's spirit finally broke, "Ricardo", he confessed.

"Ricardo Salazar"

"Dónde está este hombre, Ricardo? Where is this man, Ricardo?"

"No sé. Don't know"

Another probe, another loud scream, a gasp. He nearly passed out again. Another bucket of water splashed in his face, reviving him.

At this point, Hernando wouldn't care if they killed him.

"Dígame. Dónde está? Tell me where he is?"

"Pienso en Todos Santos. I think he's in Todos Santos"

He then passed out, slumping over in the chair he was strapped in. The restraining ropes prevented him from falling to the floor, face first.

The cruel interrogation ended.

"Take him to the hospital, Enrique. Post a guard to keep an eye on him. No visitors, he's a material witness. Don't want him bumped off. I'll call Serge immediately."

Serge Betancourt awoke with the ring of his private bedroom phone, rubbed his eyes and checked his bedside clock. It was 6:30AM, Monday morning. He'd worked late into Sunday night. He had hardly slept in the past 48 hours. He was whipped.

"Wonder who's calling?

"Hello, Juan. What's up?"…immediately recognizing his contractor's voice.

"So you caught the wounded kidnapper, good job!"

"How'd you get him to talk?"

"Good. You didn't waterboard him. You say it did not take long to break him…"

"Seriously! I don't need to hear that, Juan…"

"Yes, I understand the concept of rendition…"

"He implicated Ricardo Sandoval! Really?..."

"Now that's very interesting…"

"He told you that he's hiding out in Todos Santos?"

"Oh, he 'thinks', not affirmative…Right?"

"I understand… you dropped him off and posted a guard at the hospital… And, you detailed a squad to pick up the other two kidnappers he ID'ed in San Jose… right…OK, got it…Thanks. Nice work. See you at staff meeting later today."

He turned off the bedside light, contemplating grabbing a few more winks. The dramatic events of the last two days were exhausting. He was beat, confronted with managing one surprising incident after another.

Serge sat on the edge of his bed pondering the valuable information the 'contractors' extracted. If Sandoval is responsible for the abduction of Biff's boy, then we have an opportunity to 'kill two birds with one stone!' Good! But, what was his motive? Surely not a ransom?... An ulterior motive…? Maybe Biff was on to something, a clever diversion?... But, that implied someone tipped Sandoval, allowing him to set the abduction up. A mole?... Very complicated, confusing… Serge's emotions were signaling 'overload!'

Serge was conflicted with another problem that offended the delicate side of his sensibilities. A problem concerning 'moral relativity.'

Does the end justify the means? The 'contractors' had no constraints. The CIA had plausible deniability. How far do you push the envelope to obtain critical information?

What defines 'critical'?

What determines the 'threshold' to trigger a rendition?

An enhanced interrogation?

A kidnapping? A mission to interdict illegal weapons and drugs?

…Or, a threat of a terrorist attack on the U.S.A.?

CHAPTER TWELVE

THE DELIVERY BOY — CABO SAN LUCAS SUNDAY PM — 12 HOURS EARLIER

"**S**o tell me again, Señor Vargas, what the boy looked like. Height, weight, age, dress, mannerisms, anything you can recall, OK? Relax, you are not in trouble."

Serge proceeded to interview the Cabo Surf night clerk who received the ransom note shortly after midnight, less than 19 hours ago. The clerk had the day off, and took his family to the beach with some relatives. It was difficult, but Serge's agents finally tracked him down, requesting that he come to the Consulate to answer some questions.

Serge expected to obtain some vital information linking the ransom note to the boy, hopefully allowing him to trace it to the person who gave it to him to deliver last night. This, in turn, he anticipated would yield valuable clues leading to the perpetrators of the kidnapping.

The clerk was nervous, but accurate in his descriptions, actually quite detailed. Serge surmised that working at a famous resort cultivated the fine art of 'people watching'. This man certainly was observant, down to smallest details. That impressed Serge.

"Please continue, Señor Vargas," Serge encouraged in a polite, reassuring tone intended to allay the clerk's obvious tension. Obviously, the man had never been involved with authorities, especially regarding an abduction of a hotel's guest's child, a calamity by any measure.

"The Mexican kid was about 14 or 15 years old, I'd guess. Short curly black hair, recently cut. Nice complexion, no acne. No tattoos or scars that I noticed. Good physique, like a surfer, you know. Thin, wiry strong. I'd say the kid was maybe 5 feet tall, weighing about 100 pounds."

"How'd he dress, conduct himself?" Serge prompted.

"He had on knee length beach shorts, red with a Pez Bella logo."

"Pez Bella?" Serge asked for clarification. He knew the answer, he was testing the clerk's knowledge.

"A sailfish, the most popular game fish locally", Señor Vargas answered.

"You were describing the boy's appearance before I interrupted, sorry."

"Oh, yes. He wore a t-shirt a bit too large for him. An old one."

"How'd you know that?"

"The' Carlos and Charlie' logo was practically washed off."

"Please continue". Pardon my interruption."

"This fellow's pretty sharp", Serge reflected.

"Kid had a pleasant personality, handled himself well. I suspect he spends a lot of time around adults. Speaks proper Spanish, not much slang. Certainly not the 'gangbanger' type.

"Came in on a beat up bike. Said it took him about 45 minutes to pedal here from Cabo. He said 'barrachos' almost ran over him twice. Poor kid didn't have a light on his bike, had a reflector though," the clerk added.

"Did he say where he got the ransom note?" Serge prompted.

"Yes, as a matter of fact. I asked him. He said a 'well dressed fat man' gave the letter to him outside 'The Office' around 11 pm. The boy laughed when he described the man as 'muy gordo."

"Did the boy say what he was doing out that late at The Office? He's pretty young to be hanging out there at that hour."

"Odd that you ask. He volunteered that he works there, outside, day and night."

"For heaven's sake. Doing what?""

"This will amuse you, Señor Betancourt. He was a chatty little guy. During the day he sells cheap Mexican suntan lotion to the tourists, and at night he hawks condoms."

They shared a good laugh at this revelation.

"Please go on, Señor Vargas. This is an interesting story."

"Around 11 pm he sold his last condom and was just about to go home. Said it was a good night for sales. Usually didn't sell out before midnight."

"And…" Serge prompted, the clerk was digressing a bit.

"Tell me more, did the delivery boy have a name?"

"Let's see…I think he goes by the name, 'Claudio.'"

"Fine. Have a surname?"

"I didn't ask him and he didn't offer. Sorry."

"No problem. So, what happened next? What prevented him from going home after his last business transaction?" Serge asked sardonically.

The resort's night clerk caught Serge's tone and laughed. Serge returned a wry smile, pleased that the clerk caught his drift.

"The kid said that just as he was leaving, a well dressed fat man in a guyabara showed up, wearing white cotton gloves, holding a formal looking envelope."

"White gloves in 80 plus degree weather?" Serge exclaimed.

"Yeah, the kid got a big kick out of that! Laughing when he told me. He thought the guy about to come onto him, until he offered him fifty bucks to deliver the envelope to the resort."

"So what did he do then?"…Leading Señor Vargas along.

"You won't believe this! Claudio tried to sell him his 16 year old sister! Showed him Juanita's photo. I know it's a fact, because he showed me her picture also. Attractive teenager. It was one of those cheap passport photos, you know. Claudio promotes her as a 'knockout doll' who does tricks."

"Obviously, this industrious youngster pimps for her when he's not selling suntan lotion and condoms," Serge interjected, chuckling to himself.

"So how'd the 'fat man' respond to Claudio's offer?"

"He declined, but took her photo, address, and cell phone number. Said he had other important business to attend to, but 'maybe' on another occasion.' Not interested tonight."

"Now that's interesting. Did the delivery boy elaborate or further describe any characteristics of the fat man?"

"Let's see…Just a moment. I recall he said the man came across as 'muy rico', very rich, with fancy clothes and upper class manners. Looked about his father's age, mid fifties, but balding. Said the man was very polite. Told him if he did a good job, he'd refer other errands to him. Called them 'special deliveries.'"

"Señor Vargas, Why did the delivery boy divulge so much information to you? This is very detailed."

"I suppose he trusted me. Seemed 'street smart', sized me up to accomplish his mission. That's my best guess."

"He told me that that the envelope contained in it an urgent message for Señor Roberts. Insisted that I must see that the American guest receives it right away, not in the morning."

"For a youngster, he was quite emphatic. It is our policy to protect our guests' privacy, especially at midnight. Therefore, I quizzed him closely to determine if it was a legitimate request or concern. One serious enough to awaken a guest at that late hour. In this case, someone who had suffered a very traumatic day. The boy was unusually mature for his age. He convinced me that the message was important enough to deliver to Señor Roberts at midnight. Of course, I checked with our manager, Señor Delarosa first. Andres agreed and he personally took care of the matter before he went home."

Serge thought about this for a moment. It all seemed plausible. Vargas appeared to be a very considerate and competent night clerk. He made all the right moves.

"Just a few more questions. Did you gain the impression that the boy hangs out at The Office?"

"As a matter of fact, he told me that he spends most of his time there. If business is slow, he may hit some other ocean front bars and restaurants. He doesn't go to school. Makes good money. Helps support his family. Strikes me as a good kid."

"You seemed to have learned a lot about him in such a short time. You are quite perceptive."

"I seemed to relate to him. Reminded me of someone very close to my heart."

"How's that?"

"We lost our 15 year old son in a tragic surfing accident last year over on the Pacific coast. Up the coast from Todos Santos. Huge rogue wave drowned him and his buddy, both expert swimmers. The delivery boy reminded me a lot of him. Kindred souls, free spirits."

"Oh my! I'm so sorry I brought that up."

"You had no way of knowing."

Serge got up from his desk and shook the night clerk's his hand, and gave him a warm, heartfelt embrazo, an expression of empathy. "You've been very helpful in our investigation, Señor Vargas. You are free to go now."

After Señor Vargas left, Serge sat pensively at his desk, reflecting on their conversation, particularly its conclusion.

You never know how much heartbreak some people are dealing with. For all he knew, some 'allegoric rogue wave' had swept his kids out of his personal life into the 'Sea of Life' never to be heard from again. Serge sincerely empathized with the night clerk's loss of his son.

Serge resolved that there was no way he would allow this disaster to befall his good friend and colleague, Biff.

CHAPTER THIRTEEN

THE PICK UP – CABO SAN LUCAS SUNDAY PM

Shortly after Señor Vargas departed, Serge placed a call to his trusted bodyguard, Carlos.

"Carlos, go immediately to 'The Office' and pick up a 14 or 15 year old kid, named Claudio."

"How will I recognize him, boss?"

"He'll be selling suntan lotion and condoms outside the restaurant, or somewhere in the vicinity, maybe even marketing his sister."

"His sister?" Carlos responded in a surprised tone. Incredulous! Was his boss putting him on, or losing it?

"Yes. The delivery boy also has a night job as a pimp. A very enterprising youngster."

Serge and Carlos enjoyed a collegial laugh together. Surely Serge was joking with him, relieving some of the tension he's been under, searching for his American friend's kidnapped son.

Some people respond differently to emotional pressure. Serge certainly fell into that category. He'd observed his boss's behavior in some challenging circumstances. Serge could handle a lot of pressure, and still manage to get the job done.

"OK, Carlos, so pick up the boy and bring him in for interrogation. Handle him gently, no rough stuff. I anticipate he'll divulge some valuable information about the 'fat man' who wears a guyabara and white cotton gloves on Saturday nights in 80 degree weather. A bit eccentric, don't you think?"

"Boss, are you putting me on? C'mon!"

"I'll explain later, Carlos. It's very complicated, a bit bizarre."

"You got it, Boss. I'm on my way. Over and out."

Guess Serge wasn't kidding.

Carlos jumped into the Company jeep, heading straight for 'The Office', weaving expertly through traffic that would baffle any tourist.

He wondered about Serge. Sometimes his boss had a weird sense of humor, making it difficult to know if he was kidding or not…

"A fat man dressed for a wedding, wearing white cotton gloves around midnight, outside a laid back 'body shop' hangout on the beach?'"

"Now let me get this straight?… Pretty far out!"

CHAPTER FOURTEEN
THE FARM — TODOS SANTOS — SUNDAY EVENING

The Mexican boatman sighted the designated cove. He cut the Zodiac's outboard motor, allowing the small lifeboat to glide slowly to shore, squinting for the prearranged signal on the beach. The sun had set about an hour ago. Only a remnant of afterglow remained on the horizon to the west. He had valuable cargo and personnel aboard. It was imperative that he avoid capsizing on the treacherous, rocky shoreline. Perfecting a safe landing would test his considerable skill.

The illumination of an early arising half moon enabled him to maneuver between the numerous, dangerous reefs with their sharp projections under the ocean's surface, perilous to a rubberized craft. One ill conceived move could result in a fatal puncture, jeopardizing or aborting their mission.

Fortunately, the Pacific Ocean lived up to its name tonight, not its reputation. The sea was relatively calm, not churning, diminishing the notorious, pounding shore break. A stroke of luck for them.

"Alfredo, flash your light."

"Sí Edgar, una vez. One time."

The signal was acknowledged by two brief flashes from the beach about 150 yards to the northeast. The boatman, Edgar, altered course. He glanced aft, checking on his two passengers with their classified cargo, three green, stainless steel canisters with heavy padlocks. The containers resembled ammo boxes, Edgar thought. The two men had not uttered a word, nor taken their eyes off their precious cargo since disembarking the yacht that transported them today from Manzanillo to the present anchorage one mile off Todos Santos tonight.

"Cuidado! Careful, look out!" Edgar warned them of the imminent danger of beaching the craft at night, surrounded by reefs. Not so much the ones you could see, but those under the surface that you couldn't see. A sailor must exercise due caution.

He received no acknowledgement of his warning from the disinterested visitors. They appeared apathetic to the potential danger, almost detached, obviously preoccupied with other thoughts.

"Strange hombres," he thought. "For all I know, both are deaf and dumb! Or, just plain ignorant of the perilous path the Zodiac must negotiate. Maybe ignorance really is bliss. I've successfully done this before, but I still get tight every time I maneuver through these treacherous reefs. I have a true respect for the sea."

Edgar gunned the Zodiac's outboard motor briskly, altering their course again, slightly to the northeast towards the site of the designated signal. The riptide tended to pull the craft back out to sea. He then cut the motor, assured he had enough momentum to reach the shore. He trusted his compatriots had selected the safest landing spot for him.

Moments later, Edgar caught a small wave and glided safely ashore onto a small sandy beach in a secluded cove, a smooth landing.

"That was a bit hairy", he reflected. "All's well that ends well."

A small greeting party welcomed them. Two ominous appearing men armed with AR-15 assault rifles stood in the background at the ready should any of their plans go awry.

"Qué tal, amigos!" Ricardo Sandoval effused, as he greeted the two Cuban commandos arriving on the second leg of their clandestine assignment.

They clutched the three steel containers to their sides, next to holstered .45 caliber automatics, and nodded, not uttering a word of acknowledgement. They neglected to offer to shake hands, which pissed off Ricardo who restrained himself from a sarcastic comment. He thought to himself, "I thought the fucking Cubans spoke Spanish! Maybe they don't like Mexicans. Maybe it's a Cuban thing. Don't like how this is starting."

In the past week the two Cubans had journeyed from the Santiago Naval Base in Cuba to Vera Cruz, Mexico. Then escorted across the rural back roads of the country by Sandoval's cartel affiliates to Manzanillo. There they boarded a high speed, fifty foot yacht to "go fishing offshore for a week or so", as their permit designated for 'all intents and purposes' should the Coast Guard coincidentally stop and question them. Their papers were in order. Ricardo Sandoval left nothing to chance.

They avoided contact with their countrymen in Manzanillo, who would 'coincidentally' be conducting the annual 'sea trial' this same week of the old Soviet submarine docked for the past year at the Maritime Museum. No need to raise the slightest suspicion regarding their connection. They would meet up later.

After a concerted, second effort by Ricardo to be friendly, the two Cubans finally shook hands with him, but exchanged formalities in a rather perfunctory manner. Ricardo picked up on their indifference. He didn't know whether to attribute their discourtesy or lack of manners to a cultural difference or an obsession with their nefarious mission.

Actually, the Cubans were put off by Ricardo's sinister appearance, especially his sneer. No one had warned them.

Ricardo never made this connection in their attitude. "No matter, I'll make a fortune ferrying them to their destination. This is 'the deal of a life time!'

"Frankly, I don't give a rat's ass about their lack of cordiality or gratitude. I'll complete my commitment to facilitate their safe passage. It's not like we're fast friends or bedfellows. Why should I care?"

Ricardo quickly sized up the situation, the apparent lack of a budding relationship with the Cubans. "It is what it is."

These men were not ordinary Cubans. They were highly trained special force commandos, their expertise – Terrorism. Only they knew what the steel canisters contained, their purpose, their target and the method of accomplishing the wicked mission.

From the Cubans' standpoint, this weird looking hombre, Sandoval, was merely an instrumental middleman hired to facilitate their secure journey along established drug trafficking routes into the States. The Cuban intelligence agency had vetted him, making these arrangements. They better be accurate in their assessment of this stranger. They both disliked and distrusted him immediately. The 'sneer' set them off. It was a visceral perception, part and parcel of their intensive commando training and conditioning. If he crossed them, they'd snap his neck or blow his head off without a second's thought or an iota of remorse.

The Cubans possessed an extraordinary focus on their operation, their ingrained allegiance to Fidel Castro, and their avowed duty to rectify decades of real and perceived transgressions by the United States. Nothing would deter them. They were exceptional, if not fanatical, in their commitment to this mission. Fidel himself had imbued his confidence in them prior to their departure.

Nothing changed in the frosty relationship on the short drive to Sandoval's remote farm, several miles north of Todos Santos, near the Pacific coastline. Not a propitious beginning to their dangerous joint mission. Whether they liked it or not, success depended on mutual cooperation. The sum of the operation was greater than its parts, in essence.

"Why had no one had warned them?" the two Cubans wondered enroute to the secluded farm. Sandoval's sinister appearance disturbed them. They were surprised. They wondered...

"Can we trust this hombre? He's always got that fixed sneer on his face. He looks like a character out of an old gangster movie. Better keep a close eye on him."

Not a word was exchanged between them on the twenty minute ride. Ricardo glanced in the rear view mirror several times to observe the back seat occupants and check his security detail trailing behind in two jeeps. The stoic Cubans sat quietly, looking out at the countryside. Only on one occasion did one comment to his compadre about a coyote crossing the narrow, rutted road.

"They don't even converse with each other, strange turkeys," Ricardo noted to himself.

"Do they have coyotes in Cuba?" he wondered.

They pulled into a secluded dirt and gravel pathway off the poorly maintained paved secondary road. The two mile long path led to the remote farmhouse and barn, a bumpy ride through potholes. No outsiders ventured here. Nevertheless, Ricardo posted armed guards, not one to take chances. This precaution did not go unnoticed by the Cubans.

The farm was a clever guise, a front for the cartel's illicit operations. Ricardo achieved the desired affect by planting soy beans, corn, and citrus trees. He even hired a trusted farmer to cultivate the fields and care for the trees, a challenge in the desert climate along the coast. A few farm animals and watch dogs completed the ruse, a masterful deception.

The old barn needed repair and several good coats of paint, weathered from Pacific storms and monsoons. In stark contrast, the six bedroom farmhouse had recently been renovated, painted, and restored to its early twentieth century elegance. A safe, pleasant sanctuary for Ricardo's cartel's inner circle. Quite comfy, in fact. They maintained a housekeeper and an excellent cook. Life was good in their outback retreat.

Ricardo outsourced menial tasks and trivial pursuits to 'associates', maintaining a small close knit network of trusted aides. Ricardo was essentially a 'control freak'. Street smart, he attained the equivalence of an MBA in drug trafficking over the past forty years, a master at his trade, at the top of his game.

And, at the top of 'The Most Wanted List' in Mexico and the USA. His photo adorned many police stations, government and municipal post office walls. Nevertheless, he continued to elude the authorities time and again. His escapes baffled them.

In the old barn under bales of hay, th cartel stored bundles of marijuana, bricks of high grade cocaine from 'associates' in Mendelin, Columbia, and an arsenal of assault rifles, automatic pistols, and boxes of ammo. They stored an inventory that would make rival cartels envious.

"Consequently, Ricardo posted sentries 24/7, armed with assault rifles purchased on the open market by 'straw buyers' in Arizona and Texas where the 'wild west' attitude still prevailed, protected by the second amendment.

A couple of old farm trucks were parked nearby, gassed up for tomorrow's journey across back roads to La Paz on the Sea of Cortez, a bumpy ride over 100 miles of yet more poorly maintained roads.

Arriving at his farm, Ricardo promptly issued orders, dispatching his troops.

"Escort our guests to their quarters. Offer them a cold beverage and a snack. Explain to them our evening plans to dine and celebrate their visit tonight at Hotel California. I must walk down to the barn to check on things. We won't depart for awhile. They may take a short nap, if they wish."

After returning to the farmhouse, Ricardo attempted to give 'cordiality' another shot, announcing…

"I've arranged a special dinner celebration for you at Hotel California. The festivities will feature 'wine, women, and song', he said in his best upbeat manner.

The Cubans reacted unenthusiastically to the invitation.

"These Cubans are a real pain in the ass! You'd thought I demanded they sleep in the barn with the dogs!" he opined.

It took him and others a half hour to persuade them to leave the three special canisters in the barn under the supervision of two armed guards while they went to town. They finally relented, only because they were starved. The simple mention of a thick steak turned the trick. Off they went for a night on the town.

CHAPTER FIFTEEN

THE MYSTERY AT THE FARM — SUNDAY NIGHT

Before leaving for town, Ricardo's compulsive nature demanded that he walk down to check the barn one more time.

Meanwhile the partygoers started to load up in the three cars, ready to go to Hotel California for dinner. His men were jovial, the Cubans dour.

"Secure the premises, no napping, drinking, or goofing off. Shoot any intruders, ask questions later. Got it?" he instructed his guards at the barn. "Don't let the Cubans canisters out of your sight, OK?"

"Si, Ricardo. No problema."

The two burly sentries replied respectfully, AR-15 assault rifles slung over their shoulders, .45's holstered at their hips.

Ricardo selected these two particular guards because they had been with his cartel for over ten years without a screw up, a record of sorts in Mexico.

Ricardo's driver arrived at the barn, interrupting their conversation.

"The natives are getting restless, boss. Sorry to interrupt. The Cubans were starting to balk, still worried about those friggin' canisters of theirs. Strange dudes!"

"Got that right. OK. I'm ready to roll. Just wanted to double check on the boys. A lot of expensive contraband stored down here. We've got a BFD coming down. I can't risk any screw ups."

"I understand, boss. Hop in."

The driver, Jaime, opened the Jeep's passenger door for Ricardo, then backed up, turned around, and sped up the dirt road from the barn, fan tailing the rear wheels, raising a cloud of dust. A couple of alert barn dogs barely scurried out of the Jeep's way, barking in alarm.

"Running a little late, boss, putting the pedal to the metal. Hope Jorge has made all the arrangements."

"I'm sure he has. Jorge's quite reliable."

"Others leave already?"

"Took off about five minutes ago."

"The Cubans …?"

"Loosened up a bit after a couple of margaritas. They 're essentially rum drinkers. Not accustomed to good tequila."

Both laughed at Jaime's remark.

"Those Cubans are a piece of work! Can't get a friggin' word out of them. Not the least bit friendly. Got an attitude, hombre. Come across as mean S.O.B.'s."

"That's because they are, Jaime. They're a different breed of men."

"How's that?"

"They have an assassin mindset. They'll kill in cold blood for money or a cause. We'll kill only if threatened. They are a different kind of animal. They are on a deadly mission. That's all I can say now."

That statement seemed to satisfy Jaime's curiosity. Although, the 'deadly mission' comment puzzled him. They were in the drug and weapon trafficking business. All their missions were dangerous, potentially 'deadly', why should it be any different for the Cubans? What the Hell is Ricardo talking about?

He switched topics.

"Jorge told me that he was going over to Hotel California an hour early."

"Why?"

"Said he can't stand eating in that filthy dining room anymore. He's had it! Goin' to pay 'em fifty bucks to clean the place up. He had a laundry list. Read it to me. - "Empty the friggin' ashtrays, mop the floors with a disinfectant, air wick the room, clean the fly specks off the venetian blinds, and replace the damn light bulbs, after you dust that ridiculous fake 'Louie the 14th' chandelier!"

"You're kidding me!'

"Absolutely not. Said he felt strongly about it. Said it was about time our cartel showed a little class!"

They shared a hearty laugh.

"For fifty bucks you ought to be able to eat off the floors. Jorge is some kinda character, huh?"

"Yeah. Also, said he's making some special arrangements."

"Really?"

"Cuban cigars, Cohibas, cognac, and entertainment."

"Entertainment?"

"Jorge is bussing over some class talent from Cabo."

"Talent…?"

"Prostitutes. He said Todos Santos only had a few whores."

"What the Hell is the difference?"

"Don't know. He made the distinction. Maybe price? Risk of VD? Probably the Cabo gals are prettier, can carry a conversation, wear shoes, or something. Beats the Hell outta me."

Both laughed again. Ricardo enjoyed this discussion. It was a rare moment of relaxation for him. He'd always enjoyed Jaime's sense of humor.

"I seriously doubt Jorge will get involved with the 'ladies of the night.'" Ricardo speculated.

"Good Lord! He's not gay is he?"

"No. Jorge suffers from the 'Lolita' syndrome".

"What the Hell's that, boss?"

"Jorge prefers young girls. Basically, he's a dirty old man!" Meanwhile, back at the farm, curiosity was about to kill the cat.

"Qué crees que está en las cajas?" "What do you think is in the containers?"

"No sé." "Don't know."

The barn guards were curious, puzzled, and inquisitive as they examined the three Cuban steel canisters.

"Mira! Dice 'peligroso'!" "Look! It says 'dangerous!'"

"What do you make of that, amigo?"

"No telling what it means? Dangerous? All drugs are dangerous, if you overdose."

"What makes you so sure they contain some kind of drug?"

"Don't really know. Just guessing. Thought maybe the Cubans might be using our channels and contacts to introduce some new brand of cocaine or some kind of synthesized off label narcotic in the States. Sorta like we're their sponsors or something like that. If that's the case, knowing Ricardo, we'll get a big kickback."

"If that's the case, amigo, must be very special coke, judging from those heavy padlocks."

The older, bolder guard was a former Mexico City cat burglar, pickpocket, and an expert locksmith.

"That lock's a piece of cake!" He bragged.

"No way!"

"Bet?"

"You're on."

The older guard laughed, took a special instrument from his pocket, and started to pick the lock on canister # 3. In minutes, the lock snapped open. He glanced back at his pal and smiled, as if to say, "What'd ya think of me now?"

"No way, hombre!"

He then pried the lid open with a screwdriver, like a paint can. Inside he noted that heavy, thick plastic encased a white powder with a yellow tint.

"Looks like some special brand of cocaine sprinkled with some tobacco, probably to throw off the sniffer dogs," he joked.

"Shall we test it?"

"Won't we get in trouble?"

"Not if I carefully lock it back up. Who in the Hell would ever suspect we got this container open? We'll just sample it, not get high, OK?"

"Well...maybe. But, if we screw up, we're done. Stick a fork in us, amigo! Ricardo will kill us!"

"They won't be back from town for hours. This will take about ten minutes."

"OK, I guess, but it really worries me that we'll get caught not doing our job."

"You're such a woozy."

"Not really, I've got five kids and can't afford to lose my job."

"I promise you it'll be OK."

He made a small slit with his pocket knife in an inconspicuous edge of the thick plastic envelope where no one would notice it, even if it occurred to them.

He licked his finger and stuck it in the powder, then snorted it and tasted it. He sneezed, blowing the fine powder across the barn in a small white cloud.

"What do you think?"

"Como mierda!" "Like shit!"

"Maybe it's just for snorting. Let me try it, OK?"

"Could be the case. I'll give it another shot."

They both gave it a try, filling their palms with a large spoonful of fine powder to snort. Both were very disappointed, turning up their noses in a distasteful expression. The powder triggered an episode of uncontrollable sneezing. The strong sea breeze coming though the barn door aerosoled the powder everywhere in the vicinity.

Two barn dogs ten feet away joined the sneezing attack.

"How're they going to market this crap? It will ruin our good street rep. We push only the best stuff, amigo. Once the word gets around, we're done. After a lot of bad mouthing, our clients will shop elsewhere!"

"Bet your sweet ass! Close it up before I get sick. I can't stop sneezing! How'd Ricardo get taken in on this lousy deal? Once he samples it, heads will roll."

"Gonna be a lot of pissed off addicts and pushers in the U.S. when they buy this Cuban shit! Those Cuban bastards pulled one over on Ricardo. That takes some doin!"

"You're right, but there's no way we can warn him. He'll kill us for tampering. I agree, it's going to give our cartel a bad name. Let me close this container so no one will ever suspect that I tampered with it."

They had a big investment to protect.

The moon lit the pathway. Ricardo was in a self congratulatory mood. A bit tipsy.

He remarked, It's unusual that no dogs are greeting us, begging for a scrap of left ofver food."

The Cubans ignored his comment, which again annoyed him.

"Why doesn't that surprise me? Just treated them to a lavish dinner party and the ungrateful bastards can't even acknowledge a simple fucking comment about dogs. Everybody loves dogs except these uptight barbarians. My barber is more refined!"

The Cubans really pissed off Ricardo. He restrained himself from telling them to 'fuck off, the deal's off!' but the 25 million dollar payoff dissuaded him. He bit his tongue and marched on.

As they approached the barn he became apprehensive. He specifically nstructed one sentry to remain outside, the other inside.

"WTF! No guard, no watch dogs, nada! I suppose they fell asleep inside the barn despite my orders."

One hundred yards later they entered the barn. The horrific sight blew them away!

His two guards lay sprawled face down near the green canisters and the contraband, their rifles abandoned a few feet away. Nearby, two dogs lay rolled over, deader than doornails. Ricardo noticed three dead rats fifteen feet away. He quickly surveyed the scene. No sign of a struggle. No disarray of the barn or its contents.

"What the Hell?" He rushed to check his sentries, lying on the barn floor.

The Cubans rushed to examine the special canisters entrusted to them, almost panicking that they had failed in their mission. They exchanged a few hushed words as they ascertained the locks and lids were intact. No evidence of tampering. All three occupied the same exact order and position as when they departed to town about six hours ago. They breathed a sigh of relief.

Ricardo rolled over the bodies of the two guards so he could check their carotid pulse in their neck and further examine them for any clue to their demise.

Dismayed, he palpated no pulse, confirming his first impression. He observed no evidence of trauma on close examination. They were not the least bit disheveled. Absolutely, there was no apparent cause of death.

The barn appeared tidy, just as they'd left it. Not one sign of intrusion or a fight to the finish. Ricardo knew these two men would not have gone down without a violent struggle. Without an apparent explanation, both were now stone dead!

The Cubans were just as mystified, looking at him with a puzzled expression, but content their assignment had not been compromised. No one had messed with the containers.

One posed a rare question, "Que pasó?" "What happened?"

"No sé!" "Don't know!" Ricardo exclaimed, shrugging his shoulders in disbelief. Astounded!

He appeared a bit pale, drained by the bizarre experience.

No one had a clue! The barn mystery unsolved.

Suddenly, Ricardo sneezed several times.

The Cubans just stared at him, reluctant to ask God to bless him.

"We'll have to change our plans. We must leave tonight as soon as possible for La Paz. Let's arouse the others, pack up, and move out.

Ricardo experienced a sense of apprehension bordering on panic. He had premonition, a dread that whoever did this would soon return. Would they suffer the same mysterious fate? Anxiety filled him. Would the mission fail? A year of meticulous planning go unfulfilled? The lucrative mission go down the drain?

"I suggest you stay here, on guard, while I summon the others. Maybe one of them can unravel this supernatural event."

It was an unnecessary suggestion. No way the Cubans would leave their canisters unattended again, sensing they'd just dodged a bullet. They picked them up and lugged them to the farmhouse, ignoring Ricardo's suggestion.

Ricardo ran back to the farmhouse, got everyone out of bed, dressed, and down to the barn to evaluate the macabre scene.

The cartel sobered up quickly as they surveyed the surreal barn scene. Was it a figment of their imagination? A bad trip? An illusion? It was simply unreal!

Puzzled, they collectively reached the same conclusion that there was no plausible explanation for the barn deaths, men and animals. The mystery possessed an occult aspect. It presented an enigma beyond anyone's wildest imagination.

Ricardo started speculating that the CIA and Biff Roberts might be involved in this mystery, but quickly dismissed the thought as irrational, probably paranoid.

"Something bad has happened here, forcing a change in plans. As soon as you pack up, we're outta here. Put the Zodiac under the bales of hay with our shipment. Ask the Cubans where they want to put their special canisters."

It was still dark, an hour or so before dawn. No one spoke, stunned in a state of emotional shock.

Finally one of the men asked, "Shall we bury them, Ricardo?"

"Just leave the bodies here as they are. Don't have time for a funeral," Ricardo commanded. "Sorry…If the authorities find them here, they will be just as puzzled as we are. Meanwhile, we will be miles away."

Everyone hustled to load up the farm truck and haul ass out of here, spooked by the barn mystery. They agreed, "why take a chance?"

It was conceivable the culprits would soon return to the scene of the crime.

No need to tempt fate. What if whoever did this returned before they had a good head start up the road to La Paz?

As a precaution, Ricardo picked two of his cartel, armed with assault rifles, to stay behind while they escaped.

"Guard the barn 'til noon. Then you can take off. I know where to contact you for your next job. As soon as we leave, go over the barn with a fine tooth comb, checking thoroughly for any clues, so we can pay back the bastards who did this, OK? I checked the bodies, but nothing else, so look around real good. After your inspection, stand guard outside the barn and shoot anything that comes near! Got it?"

"Got it, boss."

CHAPTER SIXTEEN
THE HANDSHAKE AGREEMENT —
MONDAY 3:30 AM

Jorge Gomez stood silently in the barn's doorway, hands in his expensive linen trousers. He looked like an elderly statesman at the Mexican parliament, observing the commotion from his detached vantage point.

He watched Ricardo's decisive actions, commanding his troops in a crisis, like a field marshal. They all snapped to his orders. Even the recalcitrant Cubans acquiesced, hustling to pack up and leave the macabre barn scene, too spooky to describe.

"That's a 'first,'" he reflected. "Even the Cubans are freaking out!"

He saw Ricardo approaching. "Now's the time…"

"Good, I have a few questions and a proposition for him before I scoot back to Cabo tonight," he thought.

"Can you fucking believe this, Jorge?"

"No, quite frankly, I cannot. It is eerie, a supernatural experience. Like a weird sci-fi cinema, Ricardo."

"You're right, amigo. I'm moving up the operation's calendar. We're outa here, now! Off to La Paz."

"Really?" Jorge commented nonchalantly, not caught up in the intense excitement.

"Got a safe house there, outside the city. Packing up…"

"I see that…"

"Coming with us?"

"No, I'm returning to Cabo shortly. I hate to complicate matters, Ricardo, but there are a few things we should briefly discuss before you leave for La Paz and the next leg of your mission."

Jorge had a forty plus year trusted relationship with him. In fact, Ricardo considered Jorge his right hand man, his secretary, and the cartel's treasurer. And, utmost, a close confidant. If he needed to clarify a few business matters, Ricardo intended take the necessary time. Jorge had never wasted one moment of his time over all these years, he enjoyed his confidence. He would honor his request, even in these dire circumstances.

"What about the Roberts boy?"

"Father Miguel will take good care of him. I'm not going to force the issue with this Roberts fellow. I've bigger fish to fry, especially considering this recent development. My good brother of the cloth bought into the 'family crisis' story, my attempts to arrange detox and rehab for the boy's father. I warned Miguel that the boy may tell them some strange stories, as a result of prolonged abuse and stress. All the child needs is a lot of T.L.C."

"What did the good padre say to that?"

"He blessed me for my compassion for my fellow man."

Both men laughed loudly at this admission.

The other men stopped packing, looking in their direction, wondering what possibly could be humorous about the present situation in the barn.

Ricardo signaled them to resume packing, and picked up the conversation where he left off.

"Jorge, by the time…"

He sneezed again. "Pardon me. Must be allergic to some dust in the barn, same thing happened awhile ago."

"By the time the Mexican authorities and the CIA figure it all out, we'll be celebrating our jackpot up in Rocky Point. We're talking a big time pay out, serious money, Jorge."

Jorge listened intently. He was the only cartel member who knew the intricate details of the clever operation involving the Cubans. Ricardo requested his input on several occasions during the past year.

Only Ricardo had the 'cajones' to take on the top secret Cuban project, 'Cabo Caper'. The Cubans discovered Sandoval's 'ballsy' traits last year in Guadalajara, during their vetting process. That is why they selected him, not solely on the basis of his outstanding cartel track record.

The operation constituted an ingenious plot with multiple contingency plans. Distilled, all the cartel had to do was to deliver the Cubans and their classified cargo to the designated rendezvous spots on time. On the surface it sounded simple. Below the surface, significant risks existed. Ricardo recognized the stakes, Jorge the odds.

Ricardo resumed clarifying the boy's status.

"I'm certain the authorities will eventually find the boy unharmed at the church. Roberts is a smart cookie. Meanwhile, the boy's in good hands, receiving loving care. I understand he's a spunky kid."

"So far our abduction diversion has been successful. We've got Roberts sweating it out. Instead of focusing on interdicting our mission, he's concentrating on rescuing his son with his sidekick from the Consulate, Serge…what's his name…?"

"Betancourt," Jorge informed him.

"How much does Roberts know regarding our mission? Think he grasps the complexity of our caper? It's layered like an onion," Jorge enquired.

"I seriously doubt he has ever encountered a secret mission within a mission. He's concentrating on taking down our drug and weapon trafficking transactions. I'm sure he is aware of the new wrinkle involving weapon trafficking, financed by cocaine and marijuana profits. But, there is no way that he has an inkling of the Cuban connection."

"We're enjoying excellent profit margins. Should be sustainable for quite awhile," Jorge interjected. "Why even deal with the Cubans? It's risky!"

"The Cuban deal will dwarf our operations. If I pull it off, I'm hanging it up, Jorge. Tonight's incident just convinced me. It's getting spooky. Time for me to move on. The party is over. It was a great run. I'm bailing.'"

Jorge just looked him in the eye, assessing his sincerity.

"What about our business? The boys in the cartel? Without you, how can we function?"

"Tell you what, Jorge. I'm confident that you are quite capable of managing the business. I'll sell you the entire operation for one million dollars, no strings attached, absolutely no contingencies."

Jorge thought long and hard, contemplating the exceptional offer, a once in a lifetime opportunity.

"My cut for the Cuban deal is one mil. Are you willing to accept that as payment? Consider it in 'escrow'?"

"Sure. You got a deal, Jorge. The close friends sealed the deal with a warm handshake and traditional embrazo."

Both had every intention of honoring the agreement. It was a sad ending to a solid four decade relationship. Both realized they may never meet again, but refrained from expressing their deep emotional appreciation and mutual respect for each other. That would represent simply unacceptable social behavior, not condoned in the macho cartel culture.

The men witnessed this exchange, stopped loading the truck, wondering what the hell was going on?

Ricardo signaled them to carry on with their work.

Jorge started walking up the path towards his car.

"Where you going, Jorge?"

"Cabo San Lucas."

"It's well past three am, hombre. What's up?"

Jorge turned, laughed and replied, "No matter. Got a hot date with a young chick named, Juanita."

CHAPTER SEVENTEEN

THE STAKE OUT – CABO MARINA APARTMENTS – 5:30 AM MONDAY

"**A**nything happening?"

"Not yet. Juanita's apartment is # 28, over there on ground level." He points in that direction. Fancy digs for a teenager, living in the toney harbor view section."

"Ritzy part of town. Business must be good… So, no sign of him?"

"No show by the 'fat man' that the delivery boy described so well to us this afternoon. I've been here all night, Roberto. Not a sign. The kid was pretty sharp, don't you think?"

"I agree, Pedro. Kid's got his act together. Very cooperative. Judging from the information our detectives gathered later today, the boy portrayed the 'fat man' to a tee. Not bad for a 15 year old."

"With that accurate description, it was easy to track down his name, Jorge Gomez. But, unfortunately, they discovered no address for him. Seems Gomez comes and goes mysteriously. Sometimes for weeks. No rap sheet, no job, no known associates. His source of income is very puzzling. When he's in town, he's a big spender, a high flyer. Also, a big tipper. All the maître de's at the top hot spots identified him instantly. 'Big man' around town, literally and figuratively."

Both chuckled at Roberto's aspersion. The 'fat man' presented an enigma. How much valuable information would he divulge?

"It makes it all the more urgent to nab him. He is the key to tracking down the kidnappers. Supposedly, Gomez has a predilection for young girls. Have you seen Juanita?"

"Came home about midnight. Good looking young chick. Tourists must go wild," Pedro replied.

"A little young, don't you think?"

"I'll tell you, Roberto, these teenagers mature so quickly these days. I can't tell some 16 year olds from those who are 21. Juanita is well developed. She dresses well. Very attractive youngster."

"Got a point, but Gomez is a local guy. S.O.B. shouldn't be fooling around with prostitutes that young. Whippy behavior, he oughta know better."

"Maybe he's sick. Serge says he has a predilection for young girls, some kind of syndrome…"

'You're right, he's sick! I've got a 16 year old daughter. If he messed with her, I'd cut his balls off!"

"I bet he would!" Pedro thought. "Roberto can be a real mean S.O.B. when he gets riled up."

"Speak of the devil…there he is now approaching her door. Dressed like he's been at a wedding."

"Must be horny, its 5:30 am!"

"Got everything?"

"Got it. Ready to roll?"

"Si, amigo…"

"Wait until he reaches the door, just before he rings the bell, OK? Timing is everything. Stay cool, amigo!"

These two Mexican agents were CIA "Contractors", hired for "special" jobs. And, Serge had ordered this "special" job. They were pro's at extracting vital information. The agents gave "enhanced interrogation" a special meaning. Bound by no constraints or conventions, they got the job done expeditiously, while the Company maintained "plausible deniability," a convenient outsourcing arrangement.

"Win- win," as Serge rationalized the operation. These Mexican agents were valuable assets, without restraints. The high stakes involved in this situation justified extraordinary action. They must rescue Biffs' son, and bring down the nefarious cartel facilitating the Cuban terrorist plot that the NSA intercepts recently uncovered.

In Serge's assessment, this decision passed the moral litmus test. If these extreme circumstances did not rectify, justify, or reconcile the age old moral dilemma, nothing did.

"Fuck it! I'm authorizing this action."

With that decision, Serge dispatched these two agents who were about to alter Jorge Gomez' life forever. The Cabo marina stakeout approached culmination.

"With the stealth of predator cats, the agents slid from their secluded observation post in the nearby, thick bougainvillea, onto the ledge, sneaking up behind their unsuspecting target.

Before he could ring the doorbell, the strongmen jumped him from behind. Roberto roughly put Jorge in a strong hold, covering his mouth with a wash cloth soaked in chloroform to prevent a yell. Simultaneously, Pedro slammed a needle into Jorge's shoulder, injecting a full syringe of Ketamine, a fast acting, short duration tranquilizer.

It was a well rehearsed exercise, professionally executed in less than a minute. The agents were experts in the craft of abduction, and takedowns. Jorge was now their captive.

Jorge felt the sudden, sharp stab in his shoulder. He struggled to no avail. He was clearly overpowered by the surprise assault. He tried to scream for help, but the odorous, wet cloth thwarted his effort. In fact, it made him nauseous, woozy. He experienced a sinking sensation.

"Who the Hell were these thugs? Where did they come from?" Then, Jorge sensed he was about to pass out. That was his last thought.

Jorge slumped to the doorsill in a drug induced stupor.

The agents slipped a burlap bag over the captive's head and bound his extremities with rope.

"Bring the van up to the curb, he's too frigging heavy to carry any distance."

Even then it was a chore for them to lug the limp body twenty yards to the van. At this hour the streets were deserted. With considerable effort they managed to hoist Jorge into the back of the van.

"Holy shit, he's a heavy S.O.B!" Pedro swore.

"Hate to mess up his elegant guyabara," Roberto commented sarcastically.

Both men guffawed, disrespectful of Jorge. They scorned pedophiles.

"This guy's a Mexican, no excuse. Tourists maybe, if they are drunk out of their minds," Roberto commented.

"I agree regarding the tourists. They have no clue how old some of these gals are."

"May not care. It's difficult to reason with a man with a buzz on."

"Yeah. Especially, if he has a hard on!"

Pedro's last statement broke them up. They drove off laughing at the hilarious remark.

CHAPTER EIGHTEEN
THE RENDITION — MONDAY 6 AM

Less than a half hour later, Jorge woke up, groggy, naked, and strapped into a sturdy wooden chair too small for his large frame. His buttocks hung over the edge. His scrotum dangled over the front of the heavy chair. He was disoriented, the room greeted him ominously, pitch black, cold, and damp.

A wave of intense anxiety swept over him. He shivered, his pulse raced, alarmed that he could hear rats scurrying around. Stark fear gripped Jorge.

Was he captive in some dungeon? What was going on? How did he get here? Landing in this precarious predicament?

The reaction to the Ketamine injection impaired his recall and cognitive function. The drug is a dissociative anesthetic. Pharmaceutically induced confusion dominated his fragmented thought process. Basically, Jorge was spaced out, incapable of consistent, coherent thought.

"What's going to happen to me next?". He felt helpless. In fact, he was.

Apprehension aggravated his pitiful situation. Jorge sank into deep despair. He felt like a trapped animal.

Just a couple of hours ago, he was on top of the world, inheriting the cartel's lucrative business. Now he was at the bottom of the pit, not knowing what the future held for him.

This bizarre turn of events deeply disturbed him, "Holy shit! What happened? What the Hell is this all about?"

Upstairs : "It's 6 am, Roberto. Let's check on him. He should be coming around."

The two Mexican contractors went to the basement door of the safe house. Roberto hit the light switch.

The sudden illumination blinded Jorge. A single 150 watt bulb dangled above his head suspended by a cord from the ceiling. The glare spooked the rats that scattered to the far corner of the basement. Another wave of terror coursed through him, he trembled with fright.

Jorge squinted, trying to accommodate to the bright glare after being in pitch black darkness. He attempted to orient himself, focus on his stark surroundings.

Indeed, he seemed to be in a dungeon, a bare, small rectangular room with concrete floors and cinder block walls. Only the light bulb and the chair he was strapped in broke the austere, dreary monotony of the vacant room. He was imprisoned.

"Am I hallucinating? Where am I? How'd I get here? Why am I bound in this chair, stark naked?" He muttered aloud, his thoughts fleeting and fragmented.

Suddenly, he realized that he was not alone. He heard laughter at his remarks, and approaching footsteps on the stairs at the far end of the room.

"Uh oh, now what?" He experienced another sensation of panic, reaching a new level of fear of the unknown.

Moments later two gnarly, unshaven Mexican men confronted him with a menacing look on their face. Their attitude defined meanness, their demeanor malice.

Without fanfare, the older captor took his cigarillo from his lips, casually blew its smoke without passion into Jorge's face. He then stubbed it out on Jorge's wrist to establish the tone of intimidation he required for this enhanced interrogation.

"Jesus Christo, hombre! Loco?" Jorge swore, inferring the assaulter was crazy, as he yelled in pain.

"O K, Jorge, Tengo preguntas …" I've got questions…"

Jorge could feel his heart pounding, his mouth dry, anticipating this heartless inquisitor's threats and actions.

He did not wait long. The meanest looking captor took out a large Bowie knife and made a production of sharpening it close to him where he not only saw it, but heard it.

"Holy shit!"

"You're a sick man, Jorge. Fucking around with young girls." he sneered. He brandished the knife before him.

Despite the cold, damp basement, beads of sweat covered Jorge's forehead.

"Who is this madman? What does he intend to do with that big knife?"

He shivered with fright. This must be unreal, a nightmare. His memory was just returning, as the Ketamine started to wear off.

He'd left the farm just before 4 am; arrived at Juanita's apartment around 5:15, then someone grabbed him from behind…that's all he recalled. Next, he woke up here, bound, naked, and imprisoned in a cold, pitch black basement.

Now, he faced an unknown fate at the hands of this violent maggot.

Jorge briefly struggled. Useless, the bonds tightly constricted him to the heavy wooden chair.

"Ahora, preguntas…" Roberto said in a sinister tone, "Now questions."

"Preguntas, Señor?" Jorge asked in a fragile tone.

"Dónde está su amigo, Ricardo Sandoval?" "Where is your friend, Ricardo Sandoval?"

Jorge hesitated, thinking Ricardo should be loaded up and headed out by now. He could afford to give up some limited information to this mad dog. By the time the information he divulged reached the interrogator's handlers, Ricardo would be in La Paz with the contraband. If the information traveled through the Consulate, Ricardo would be tipped off and take further evasive action. No way could the authorities head off their special shipment. Jorge attempted to play the part of the reluctant confessor.

"Last I heard, he was in Todos Santos"

"Where in Todos Santos?"

Jorge hesitated momentarily. "Hotel California," he said in an unconvincing tone.

"Are you kidding me? A 'Most Wanted' criminal staying at a tourist hotel? Surely, you don't think I'm buying that story! You insult my intelligence, Jorge. Not a good start to my interrogation."

Roberto approached him and menacingly balanced his victim's scrotum on the blunt edge of his hunting knife, jiggling it up and down, laughing scornfully.

"How 'bout this package, Pedro?"

Jorge reflexively flinched and cried, "Please! Please…don't!"

"Dígame la verdad!" Tell me the truth!"

Frightened beyond belief at what may transpire next, Jorge Started spilling the beans, giving detailed directions to Ricardo's farm outside of Todos Santos.

He hoped this would satisfy this sadist, fearful of what he may ask or do next. "You have been helpful to this point, Jorge," Juan again jiggled the captive's scrotum on the knife, further terrifying him. The cold knife blade sent chills down his spine.

Jorge involuntarily urinated, the stream running down his legs, pooling at his bare feet on the cold concrete floor.

His abductors laughed derisively with brutal scorn.

"Acting like a whipped yard dog puppy!" Roberto scoffed, further humiliating Jorge, another critical step in breaking him.

Jorge shook with anxiety, sinking into despair. It was obvious no mercy awaited him, no pity afforded him.

"Listen, Jorge. Did you give the ransom note and money to the 'delivery boy' last Saturday night to take to Cabo Surf?"

Even under extreme duress, Jorge began to recover his cognitive faculties, as the Ketamine dissipated in his blood stream. He hesitated, momentarily, contemplating his narrow options. Admitting to this question implicated him in the kidnapping, leading to a long Mexican jail sentence. Somehow he must obfuscate the transaction.

Roberto became impatient and viciously demanded, "Did you?"

Jorge still hesitated, trying to come up with a diversion. A big mistake.

"Perhaps this will refresh your memory," Roberto said emphatically.

Roberto suddenly nicked Jorge's scrotum with the razor sharp tip of his hunting knife.

Jorge's scream pierced the damp, humid air of the basement, bouncing off the small room's walls.

Pedro winced, Roberto was getting excessively rough, over the top.

Blood ran down Jorge's legs, mixing in the pool of urine at feet. It was an ugly sight to even a hardened, veteran agent.

"This sick bastard is showing no compassion. He's ruthless!"

Jorge thought, as he almost passed out, panting, begging for mercy.

"Is this sadistic S.O.B. going to emasculate me?" He sensed a new level of panic about to overwhelm him.

"You know, Jorge, there is a cure for pedophilia…"

"Oh no! Please don't castrate me!"

Pedro was becoming uncomfortable, questioning his partner's intent and intensity. Surely he wouldn't get that carried away, "I hope that he's just threatening the target very convincingly, to break him"

The brutal scene was so convincing that Roberto was even fooling him. He'd never observed him acting this insanely aggressive. Excessive, even by their lax coercive standards.

He predicted Jorge would soon break. Experienced special force operatives would fold under this savage pressure. Jorge was a mere dilettante.

"OK, Jorge. If you cooperate, answering all my questions promptly, I won't castrate you. But, if you dare fuck with me, I won't hesitate to cut your balls off! Don't test me," he growled.

For emphasis, he pricked Jorge's scrotum again, eliciting another scream, another plea to cease this line of interrogation.

It was torture!

"Let me remind you, if I castrate you, you will either bleed to death slowly, or, if you survive, be a eunuch the rest of your life!"

By this time, Jorge was sobbing, resigned to his fate, plaintively begging for pity. He'd tell them whatever they wanted to know.

"Good God, please…" crying for mercy.

Pedro was recording the interrogation for evidence. He thought he might have to edit it. This was brutal beyond the pale!

"OK, let's start again, now that we have an understanding," Roberto said sarcastically.

"Did you give the ransom note to the 'delivery boy', Claudio, at the 'Office'?"

"Sí, Señor."

"Did you wear white cotton gloves to avoid fingerprints on the parchment paper note?"

"Sí, Señor."

"How did you know Mr. Robert's and his family were in Cabo? Staying in suite #22 at the Cabo Surf resort?"

Jorge paused too long. Juan impatiently pricked his scrotum a third time, another scream, followed by another plea to 'Stop it for God's sake!" Jorge briefly passed out.

Roberto slapped him across his face, reviving him.

"Roberto, you're killing him. Back off a little, OK, hombre?"

"Let me handle this, Pedro," he said curtly.

"Did you get my question, Fat man?" he said in a derogatory tone.

"Si, Ricardo Sandoval told me. He typed the ransom note and the address."

"Where did he get the fancy stationery?"

"I really don't know, Señor." I'm telling the truth. Please don't cut me again! I swear to God."

Roberto was convinced Jorge wouldn't risk his balls to cover up at this point.

That was a safe bet.

Pedro continued recording, wondering where all this was going. Roberto was certainly extracting vital information, but was he on the verge of killing this guy?

"Where is the boy?"

"Which boy?"

"The Roberts boy they kidnapped. Don't mess with me, Jorge!" Juan growled impatiently.

"Sorry. I thought you meant the 'office' boy."

Juan let that one go… "Where is the Roberts boy?"

He moved the knife threatening close, towards Jorge's scrotum.

"The boy's location? Tell me now!"

"In Todos Santos. In the custody of Ricardo's brother."

"His brother?"

"Father Miguel, at the Catholic church in Todos Santos, I suppose. I'm not certain," risking being evasive, hedging despite the beating and grilling to which he'd been subjected. Jorge could barely hang on.

"You better not be lying to me. If your story doesn't pan out, I'll come to your jail cell and castrate you!"

Jorge had no doubts that he would be good to his threatening words. He was dealing with a 'sadistic madman', a bad character combination.

"OK, next question. What's the deal with the Cubans? What's in the canisters?"

This question shocked Jorge.

"How in the Hell did this guy know about that? It was 'top secret', only he and Ricardo knew the general details. The Cubans were on 'a need to know' basis, playing it close to the vest. He had no clue regarding the contents of the canisters."

"Honestly, I don't know the details, just a few generalities."

"Tell me what you do know. Don't lie to me."

He wouldn't dare risk another cut by this deranged mad dog.

"Essentially, they've hired us to escort them up north, hook them up with our best coyote to cross the desert to the States."

"Destination?"

"Don't know."

"What's in the canisters?"

"No clue. I've told you all I know, believe me."

Roberto reflected, "I've intimidated and broken him. He wouldn't lie at this point."

He switched to his 'good cop' routine."

"You are being very cooperative now, Jorge. Just a few more questions and we will drop you off at the E.R. for medical care. Your scrotum will heal nicely. We will tell the Doctor we found you by the roadside, high on narcotics, naked, and bleeding from climbing over a barb wire fence, hallucinating that a bull was chasing you.

They will run a drug panel to confirm our story. To make it verifiable, Pedro will soon inject you with 15 mgm of morphine sulfate. You'll be stoned when we drop you off at the E. R. No one will believe your story about what transpired here tonight. An associate will pick you up after discharge, so don't try to escape, or warn Sandoval. We've got you covered.

"Clever bastards. They thought this out. At least they are not planning to kill me. Yet…"

"Final questions, Jorge…"

"How did Sandoval know of the Roberts' family plans? All the fine details?" His classified status with our U.S. consulate here?"

Without hesitation, Jorge responded. He needed to get out of here with his family jewels intact. Away from this cruel madman.

"Ricardo has a reliable informant inside the Consulate who keeps him posted of any positive threat."

"Name?"

"Not the slightest inkling."

"Lying to me?"… brandishing the knife close to Jorge's scrotum…

"Believe me. I'd tell you, if I knew."

Jorge was emotionally drained and physically exhausted. He couldn't take much more. No more games.

Roberto examined Jorge's demeanor, carefully trying to detect a lie. He glanced at Pedro for confirmation, brandishing his intimidating knife once again.

"What d' ya think?"

Pedro looks up from preparing a syringe of morphine for injection into Jorge.

"I think he prizes his balls. I'd say he's telling the truth, Roberto."

Roberto whipped the knife off on Jorge's thigh, then ceremoniously sheathed it.

Jorge flinched, Roberto laughed scornfully.

"No more questions, you sorry piece of shit!"

CHAPTER NINETEEN

THE UPDATE — THE US CONSULATE CABO — SUNDAY PM - 12 HOURS EARLIER

"I know it's been tough on you and your wife, Biff. But, it's only approaching early Sunday evening and we are making strides in our investigation.

"I'm sweating it, pal. Wife's a nervous wreck. She's usually rock solid in a crisis."

"Gotta admit, Biff, this isn't a 'routine crisis', if there is such a thing."

"Listen, got some important leads. Late this afternoon, we tracked down the delivery boy who implicated a middle age fat man hiring him to deliver the ransom note. Works with Sandoval, we think from our other sources, but can't confirm it. Keeps a clean record, covers his trail. Sharp dressing dude by the name of Jorge Gomez our detectives say. High flyer around town, hustles young chicks. I mean statutory rape young. May be a pedophile, or certainly he's suffering from the 'Lolita syndrome.'

"The delivery boy offered to sell him his 16 year old sister last night, but he declined. Said he was busy, but took her card, photo, and cell number for future reference."

"She maintains a fancy apartment over by the marina."

"Business must be good," Biff observed.

"Got that right."

"We're staking out her apartment. If the fat man shows up, we'll nab him."

"OK, Biff, gotta a second lead. We hope to pick up that guy you shot at a medical dispensary no later than tonight. He can't last much longer without seeking medical attention for his gunshot wound, I predict. We've got all facilities staked out."

"Really, good move!" Serge.

"I figure he will confess who hired him and his two buddies to kidnap your boy through an intermediary, whose description I bet will fit Jorge Gomez, 'fat, bald, middle age, sporting a guyabara."

"Must attend a lot of weddings," Biff joked. Serge chuckled.

"I'm sure glad you wounded one kidnapper. That will soon pay off."

"I'm not sorry to hear that," Biff commented sarcastically. "If he didn't have my son in his arms, he'd be dead. That was the only safe shot I had to cause him to drop my boy. Unfortunately, they escaped."

"You were in a tough bind. At least you winged him, forcing him to seek medical attention. That will set up his capture and give us other valuable leads, Biff."

"This dude will be captured, and will ID the other two kidnappers, where they hang out, the whole nine yards. We'll get 'em, Biff. Give you 10 to 1 odds all will be in jail by tonight, or tomorrow."

"I'd never bet against you, pal."

"OK, our forensic team thinks the ransom note may have originated at the Catholic church in Todos Santos. If so, Sandoval's gang may be hanging out over on the coast."

"Todos Santos?"

"It is a small town over on the Pacific coast, Biff. Off the tourists' beaten path, except for one iconic establishment. Ever heard of the Hotel California?"

"The one in the 'Eagles' famous song?"

"Yes, the one and only. We're in the process of setting up a 24/7 stakeout team. Photo and Bio briefing tonight so they recognize all the cartel players in the program."

"Good show, Serge."

"The bartender is on board as an informant. Says they frequent the hotel. Identified the photos right away."

"A word of caution, Serge. If they are regulars, they probably have the bartender already on the payroll as a lookout. I wouldn't be surprised if he's tipped off Sandoval, earning a tidy bonus. Cartels like Sandoval's leave little to chance. Don't mean to rain on your parade, but I've been burned by double-dealers."

"Good point. I'll take it under advisement."

"This is extremely valuable information you obtained in such a small time frame, Serge. How'd you come by it?"

"You don't want to know, Biff."

"Outsourcing your 'special' jobs, Serge?" a rhetorical question.

"Gotta have plausible deniability, Biff. You know the rendition routine."

Biff decided not to go there. He changed the conversation.

"Looks like we're getting somewhere, Serge. Nice work by your team."

"That's not all, Biff. Get back to considering the ransom note. The font and peculiar parchment quality led us to start checking every church in Cabo, La Paz, and San Jose. My bodyguard, Carlos, and a forensic expert are already enroute to Todos Santos to visit the Catholic church there in view of the current leads we obtained during our afternoon interrogations."

"If it's credible evidence, Sandoval conceivably used the local church typewriter and stationery to produce the ransom note. This could be a game breaker, Biff. Gomez represents the middleman who hires the delivery boy to transport the note to Cabo Surf, a nice three step maneuver to obfuscate the trail to the note's originator."

"We've lucked out so far with our interrogations. If we nab Jorge Gomez, we'll have not only a vital link to Sandoval, but a significant lead to your son and the cartel's Cuban caper. It could all come together quite nicely, Biff."

"Clever stunt!"

"We're dealing with sharp criminals, don't you agree?"

"Yes, but one other thing. Explain to me how these characters knew I was here in Mexico, where I was staying with my family? How'd they know my son would be surfing yesterday morning"

"I sent you an electronic message over a secure consulate back channel about a week ago. Detailed all my plans. Did you receive it?"

"No, Biff, I did not. I thought it was odd that you arrived a few days early. I would have assigned a security team and picked you up at the airport. That would have averted this catastrophe."

"I thought as much. You're not the kind of guy who spaces important matters. So, I conclude that someone with access to classified transmissions at your consulate intercepted the message, did not inform you, but tipped off Sandoval who could plan the kidnapping without any concern of dealing with a security detail protecting my family. My son essentially, was a 'sitting duck.'

"I was shaving, got to the balcony too late to shoot the abductors at close range. I couldn't risk many shots with my son in their possession. I'd liked to have emptied my clip on those bastards."

"The only reasonable explanation to me, Serge, as I've told you, is that you have a well placed 'mole', a spy, in your consulate. For all I know, the mole keeps Sandoval informed of any potential threat."

"That would explain a lot of screw ups, Biff! I'm in the process of checking it out."

"My son's abduction may be retribution for my role in the San Francisco bust involving Sandoval back in '69. Or, it may be a clever diversionary tactic to distract us from our joint mission to interdict Sandoval's cartel's business. Maybe Sandoval thinks we can't focus on multiple problems simultaneously, while he pulls off some big deal with the Cubans."

"Your explanation is compelling and plausible. Only six people at the consulate have the proper security clearance to handle back channel classified communications. All have been with me for years, all very trustworthy. I'd be hard put to single one out."

"I'd suggest you lay a few traps to ferret out the traitor, increase your personal surveillance, and trust no one with your suspicions, Serge."

"Got it, pal. I'll get all over it."

"Getting back to the Cabo caper, our latest NSA intercept out of Cuba indicates the transfer of three steel canisters to Sandoval is imminent in the next few days. No specific details, but they suspect the worst case scenario, a terrorism plot. The intercept indicates a rendezvous near La Paz, and transport up the Sea of Cortez. Unfortunately, no rendezvous coordinates were designated."

"Probably they prearranged those. I assume you've set up maximum sea and air surveillance?"

"Yes, including random boardings and searches. Going to fuck up fishing this week. The coast guard will launch their entire fleet this week, day and night. Also, we plan surveillance from low flying aircraft.'

"The federales are scouring La Paz, and all ports up the seacoast, searching every nook and cranny. Hopefully, we can head 'em off, Biff. They don't know that we know what they are up to, so we have the element of surprise."

"Are you sure of that, Serge?" Biff alluded to the suspected mole.

"We are using an intensified version of our drug traffic intervention program with double the personnel in the effort. We anticipate the Cubans are taking a page out of the cartel playbook, using established smuggling routes and tactics. Gotta get 'em before they hook up with the coyote."

Why's that, Serge?"

"The desert's expansive, the best coyotes have over 20 years' experience, and the border is porous, regardless of what Homeland Security asserts."

"So, we've got to intercept them somewhere enroute, Biff. Best place to start is Todos Santos from all indications."

Serge hit the intercom.

"Alicia, notify the boys to warm up the jeep. We're heading for Todos Santos in five minutes. Contact Carlos and inform him we are on the way. We will hook up with him over there in about an hour, depending on traffic."

Obediently, Alicia notified the garage bodyguards, then called Carlos' Blackberry. He'd left earlier for Todos Santos. She sensed that something big was happening.

It was late Sunday afternoon, usually a laid back Mexican family day. For everyone to leave Cabo for Todos Santos struck her as weird. Nothing much ever happened over there in that sleepy little town.

Carlos called back in five minutes, a record response time for him. The connection was good, considering the coastal mountain range.

"What's up, Alicia?"

"Serge and Mr. Roberts are on their way over to meet up with you. I guess something big is coming down," probing for more information.

"Thanks for informing me, Alicia." Carlos ignored her comment and hung up abruptly.

A moment later she placed a call to a private cell phone number. The call went directly to voice mail. Alicia left a cryptic message.

"Heads up! The posse is on their way to Todos Santos."

She placed the phone down, sighed, and looked out her window at the clear blue sky. It was a beautiful late Sunday afternoon. She leaned on the window sill and thought, "What in the world is going to happen next?"

Next, Carlos called back in minutes with a frantic message.

"Alicia, tell Serge to hold off his trip over here until the morning. One of our forensic team just arrived with some bad news. That's why I hung up on you."

"He told me that just as he was going up and around a steep mountain curve, when an out of control farm truck loaded with pigs coming down the mountain, swerved, almost sending him over a cliff. Unfortunately, the farm truck hit the big rig trailer behind him, causing a jack knife roll over. The road is blocked on the steepest incline. Squealing pigs running all over the place. Three rear end collisions occurred behind the rolled over rig, blocking the road. A lot of injuries," he said. "It is pure chaos!"

"My God! I'll let Serge know immediately. He's on his way to the garage," Alicia responded. "I'll head him off."

"Good. I suspect it will take the authorities all night to clean up the mess. Tell Serge we should be able to hook up in the a.m. I'll monitor the cleanup project from here. The accident occurred about ten miles south of town. I'll keep you posted, Alicia. Over and out."

Alicia contacted Serge in the Consulate's underground garage. She was not surprised at his brief response, she smiled.

"WTF!" Serge exclaimed.

CHAPTER TWENTY
THE CALL - MONDAY 7:00 AM

"**S**orry to wake you up, Serge, at this early hour, but we just broke Jorge Gomez. He confessed some very interesting information. Thought you needed to know right away."

"No problem. I just drifted off after Juan called me about one half hour ago with some other leads... Up sorta late last night," Serge explained. "Fill me in..."

Two breakthrough calls in rapid succession. Things were beginning to hop! Serge turned the light back on, so he could take notes.

"Real interesting stuff! 'Game changers', in fact!" the caller reported in a very excited tone, unusual for this particular 'contractor' who rarely expressed any emotion. He had a 'hard ass' reputation.

"No problem, Roberto, shoot... give me a quick summary, OK?" Picking up on his tone.

"Apprehended him at Juanita's apartment door around 5am."

"Juanita?"... Serge was not yet fully awake after spending a late night evaluating this complex, ongoing abduction case. He was trying to pick up Roberto's trend of thought. Where was he going with this?...

"The office boy's 16 year old sister, the hooker that we staked out."

"OK, gotcha, Roberto. Now I'm on track. Continue on."

"Here's the skinny. The office boy, Claudio, is legit. His story is solid! Gomez is definitely the intermediary in the ransom note exchange. Wore white cotton gloves to avoid leaving finger prints. He admits that

Sandoval typed the ransom note on church stationery in Todos Santos. Says Sandoval maintains a 'hideout' farm northeast of town. The cartel stashes contraband in his barn, a staging area."

"Fantastic info, Roberto, I suspect Gomez did not volunteer this confidential knowledge," Serge chided him.

Roberto chuckled at Serge's inference.

"We had a friendly little discussion over a cup of tea and crumpets."

"Yeah, right, Roberto," snickering at the contractor's wry sense of humor.

"Get this, Serge. This will blow you away!"

"Sandoval's brother is the local Catholic priest, Father Miguel. Gomez says Sandoval turned the Roberts boy over to the good father and his nuns for 'safe keeping.'"

"Serge, wouldn't you think the clergy folks would put two and two together with the all the newscasts and the APB about the Roberts boy's kidnapping? Notify someone? This is sensational news. Everybody is talking about it. In fact, it has never happened before in our world famous resort. Cabo San Lucas may get a bad tourist rep outta this."

"I'm really not surprised, Roberto. Those folks live in a celestial microcosm at the Catholic Church. No TV, radio, newspapers. Live a spartan, religious life, isolated from the mainstream. There's no 'amber alert system' in Mexico, so I doubt they'd be aware of a something as rare as a kidnapping in Cabo San Lucas. I'm sure they are attending to their divine duties and taking good care of the boy, oblivious to our search efforts. I'm certain Sandoval fed Father Miguel some 'cock-and-bull' story. Being good hearted folks, I'm sure they bought into his fabrication. Their entire life is dedicated to service and care giving.

"How'd you know all about this church stuff?"

"I used to be a devote Catholic, Roberto. Even considered entering the Seminary."

"Wow! Never knew that about you! You make a good point, boss. The lack of communication with the outside world would explain it. But, now we've got a good lead on the kid. Better check the story outright away, don't you think?"

"Started to go over last night with Biff Roberts to follow the forensic lead on the ransom note, but a big rig accident blocked the road all night. Plan to give it another shot as soon as I get dressed. Carlos is already in Todos Santos investigating a lead we got from the wounded kidnapper, Hernando, regarding Sandoval 's farm hideout somewhere over there on the Pacific coast."

"OK, boss, I'll make it easy for Carlos. I'll e-mail his Blackberry the specific directions that Gomez confessed to me. The farm is remote, northwest of town, down a dirt road that is not well marked. That will make Carlos' job a piece of cake. Otherwise, it would be a 'needle in the haystack' proposition. The bad guys hang out in the boonies. Carlos could spend a couple of days searching for the farm."

"Great! That will be a big help, Roberto. Hernando's directions were vague, but I guess he'd never been there, plus he was delirious with a high fever from the infected gunshot wound. I'll contact Carlos to relay that information, as soon as you hang up. I'll give him a heads up to expect your e-mail."

"Get any other valuable facts out of Gomez?"

"As a matter of fact, two other important tidbits, Serge. Jorge 'spilled the beans '."

"He outlined the generalities of the Cuban plot, using established cartel routes and contacts to transport the three steel canisters, but obviously, Jorge was not in the loop regarding specifics. Also, he swore he didn't have a clue what's in those Cuban's containers, that remains a 'mystery', to use his word."

"Believe me, he wasn't lying. I had his full attention."

"I bet you did, Roberto", sardonically tweaking his 'special interrogator'.

Serge appreciated Roberto's terrific interrogation results, but as with Juan's results, he was conflicted with the contractors' methods, again presenting a personal dilemma of 'moral relativity' to Serge.

He had never completely resolved this inner conflict of principles, so he tended towards action that achieved pragmatic, positive outcomes, even though he still felt bad about it. There was no question that the contractors produced valuable, actionable information consistently.

That was in their 'contract'. That's what they did.

Serge's contract's major tenet demanded that he maintain national security. That was his job.

In the final analysis, only positive real world results counted. The contractors provided positive results enabling him to fulfill this sworn obligation, the methodology be damned!

In Serge's world, the matter, the nitty gritty came down to perception versus reality. He was committed to 'real world' results. He'd learned to deal with his emotional reservations long ago, not to confuse perception with reality. He'd worked through the the risk/ benefit algorithm so many times as a CIA operative that decision making in critical circumstances became second nature to him. He remained objective. National security was his job, his priority. Personal feelings about rendition must be put aside.

'Please continue, Roberto. Sorry to interrupt. I was thinking about something else."

"No problem. I understand rendition stresses you. My job is to produce solid results, so wait 'til you hear this… maybe you will change your opinion about enhanced interrogation."

"I asked him why this Cuban mission is such a BFD? What's their game plan? What's the end game with the canisters? Other than the fact that the plot involves big money for the cartel as 'escorts', Jorge did not have a clue, honestly. No inkling of the big picture, nada!"

Before Serge could comment, Roberto blurted out…

"But, here's the bombshell, Serge … Listen to this…"

"What's that?" Serge excitedly interrupted.

"Jorge told me that we have a well positioned informant in our Consulate. The 'mole' tips Sandoval of any potential threat. That's how he stays always stays a step ahead of us. We always thought it was because he was just more clever than us. Not the case, Serge. Sandoval received critical inside information on a regular basis!"

"Holy shit!" Serge exclaimed. "Who in the Hell betrayed us?"

"Jorge didn't know. It's up to us to discover the traitor."

"It gets worse, Serge. The mole divulged to Sandoval all the details of Biff Roberts' visit, vacation plans, and mission, but not to you or anyone at the Consulate!"

"WTF! Biffs' premonition was definitely correct! That allowed Sandoval to set up the Roberts kid's abduction without any protection or interference from us!" Serge thought to himself…

"Got it, Roberto. I'll get on it right away, add it to my 'To do' list!"

CHAPTER TWENTY ONE
THE OTHER CALL — MONDAY 5:30 AM

"It's Ricardo calling… Yes, I realize its 5:30 in the morning. Sorry to wake you up, but we had a sudden change in plans."

"I'll explain later…Look, it's not my problem that you whooped it up 'til 3am. Don't be so cranky, I'm paying you top dollar for this job."

"We're moving up the operation by a half day, leaving Todos Santos now…"

"Doubt there will be much traffic at this hour …Arrive around 7:30 to 8 o'clock… Yes, I'll watch for tractors on the road, Edmundo. You're starting to sound like my mother, for Christ's sake!"

"That would be great… having all the provisions on the dock ready to ship out. Don't want to hang around and attract any attention."

"Good point. A lot of fishermen at that time. …crowded dock… agree…"

"There are six of us, four Mexicans, two Cubans."

"What are the Cubans like? Ha!..."

"'Intransigent bastards' would best describe them. I can't wait to turn them over to our coyote."

"One jeep, one farm truck… OK, we'll park at the northeast end of the marina lot."

"Got it. Your boat is docked at slip 288. Northeast Pier A."

"How big is your fishing boat? …45 feet, that's good size with a lot of horsepower. Will it hold a Zodiac with an outboard motor? … Oh, in that case, we'll tow it… Listen, Edmundo, I don't give a rat's ass that it will screw up your trolling. We are towing the Zodiac, no discussion."

"Look, you'll have all afternoon and evening to fish after you drop me and the Cubans off at the island offshore."

"I know there are a lot of islands out there in the Sea of Cortez, I Google mapped our exact destination and midnight rendezvous spot. Write down these coordinates:

Latitude – 24° 08` 32" N

Longitude – 110° 18` 39" W

"Check the nautical charts with the marina commodore regarding unmarked reefs and hazards, OK?"

"The name of the island is Isla Espirito Santo… Good you know it… Dammit! I don't care about how good the Rooster fishing is, you can take the boys… Edmundo, I don't care if I' m missing the opportunity of a life time. I'm focused only on our mission… How far is it up to the next island, Isla Partida?"

"OK, just 4 or 5 miles. That is the location of our midnight rendez-vous. I want to be there early, OK?"

"Cargo? Small personal shipment, plus three steel canisters belonging to the Cubans…a little heavy. How close to the dock can we park?"

"Good. Be sure to have a couple of dollies available, OK?"

"That's a good list of provisions, lots of cold beer … No problem. I don't care how busy the dock is when we arrive. Just be ready to ship out as soon as we load up."

"I'm glad you understand… We're dressed for fishing in case some-one has staked out the marina … You guessed it, we're under a little heat, and we are 'armed and dangerous'!"

Both men shared a hearty laugh at Ricardo's dark humor."

"See you in a couple of hours."

CHAPTER TWENTY TWO
THE VERANDA – CABO SURF RESORT – MONDAY 7:30 AM

"**B**uenos días, Señor y Señora. Sorry to interrupt your breakfast, but I have an important message from Serge Betancourt.

"Excuse me, Mary Beth. I'll be right back."

Several early morning diners glanced in Biff' s direction as he got up and walked slowly to the edge of the veranda, obviously to discuss a private matter with the well dressed Mexican gentleman who just arrived.

"That guy sure has a lot of balls in the air. Can't even enjoy his breakfast," one commented to his companion.

"Hate to deal with his problems. He seems to be holding it together. Tough dude," his business associate replied.

The unfolding drama involving this imposing American and his attractive wife captivated the resort's tourists. They were fascinated with the kidnapping's outcome, and what role this man would play. At this juncture they had correctly deduced that Biff Roberts enjoyed V.I.P. status. Why? They hadn't a clue.

Biff returned to their table and bent over to quietly inform his wife of a developing situation.

"Looks like we have some credible leads, dear. We're off to Todos Santos. It took them almost all night to clear the mountain road from last evening's big rig accident. I'll keep in touch. I'm optimistic that we are on the verge of a break through."

"I hope and pray so, Biff."

She gave him a warm smile of confidence that he immediately recognized. She was definitely regaining her emotional strength and resolve, no longer weepy and at loose ends. She had only taken one Ambien in the last 24 hours.

"Yes, she's coming around, pulling it together," Biff noted.

He bent over and kissed her goodbye, then hustled to the waiting Consulate car in the parking lot.

"I'll see you soon, sweetheart."

She watched him leave without a bite of his breakfast.

Observant diners felt for her, but were hesitant to go over to console her, respecting her privacy. They could not imagine what she was going through.

"Maybe… depending how involved matters became. 'See you soon' could be hours, days, even weeks in Biff's line of work." She reflected as Biff drove off in the limo.

Thirty years of marriage had taught her reticence. She knew the demands and complexities of his profession. He could be gone for an indeterminate time.

"Whatever it takes to get the job done" was his attitude. She resigned herself to the fact that in the end, Biff would come through for her and their son. She had lost her appetite when Biff suddenly departed, but forced herself to eat some of her breakfast. She thought about their situation.

"He seemed encouraged that the new leads would be productive, I hope it will not be a 'wild goose chase.'"

She prayed several times a day that they would find Boo unharmed. Emotionally, she knew that she was recovering her positive attitude. Her religious faith bolstered her hope and confidence. "Dear God, let them find Boo."

She watched Biff's limo exit the same parking lot where Boo was snatched 48 hours ago. The terrifying image was still vivid.

"Serge apologizes that he left without you," the driver, Chico, said as he and Biff pulled out of the resort parking lot. "He got a wakeup call an hour ago and took off immediately for Todos Santos while the trail was still hot.

We'll meet up with him over there. He said to inform you that we're on the verge of a big breakthrough on two fronts, recovering your son, and tracking Ricardo Sandoval."

"Terrific! Who tipped him?"

"Serge instructed me not to discuss the source of the information with you, Señor Roberts, sorry."

"OK, I get the drift…"

Chico drove too fast for Biff's comfort. Biff observed that all Serge's consulate bodyguards drove with the verve of a bullfighter, in a nation of passionate, macho 'bullfighters' and 'bulls'. They competed on narrow two-lane roads for space, only giving way at the last minute to the matador of the moment. All Chico lacked at the wheel of the jeep was a big red cape to wave triumphantly, as his skillfully swerved back into his lane, barely missing oncoming traffic in another close call.

Dodging in and out of congested morning commute traffic, they were soon on the windy mountainous road to Todos Santos with its steep curves, switchbacks, and perilous drop-offs into ravines and arroyos below. Guard rails would be an admission of unmanliness in the national macho psyche. It was a nerve racking trip for Biff.

Chico drove with undaunted courage, much to Biff's chagrin. He now understood why it took most of the night to clear the road after yesterday's accident. Biff sighed, but restrained himself from comment. He didn't want Chico to think he was a woozy.

"I'll try to contact Serge or Carlos, Señor Roberts."

"Biff is fine with me, Chico. Please address me by my first name, OK?"

"Sí, Señor Roberts."

Biff decided to let it go. "Must be a protocol thing," he thought.

"Hola, bueno!" Carlos answered loudly.

"This is Chico. I've got Señor Roberts with me. We're about forty minutes outside town. Where are you? Where shall we meet?"

"Farm?... What farm? Sandoval's farm? OK, give me the directions. I think I've got it, but shoot it to me one more time… OK…go five miles northeast after passing through town … Describe the dirt road turn off again… OK, got it… How far down the dirt road to the farm? Three miles… OK, see ya soon."

"Sandoval's got a farm?" Biff enquired as Chico signed off the call.

"Guess so. We'll soon see." he said as he accelerated up the last big curve before the descent into Todos Santos. Crews were still cleaning up remnants of the accident. Peasants were rounding up surviving pigs, and carting off 'road kill.'

Customarily, Mexican towns have speed bumps, 'totopas', to control traffic speed flow though the busy streets full of pedestrians, carts, bikes, and animals. This refinement had not reached this sleepy village, somewhat locked in a time warp.

Chico sped through town, honking his horn to warn the unwary. Slowing down, or braking was out of the question. The town had one aged policeman and one postmaster who were having coffee at this hour. One crossed the street at their own risk.

Chico suddenly hit the brakes, barely avoiding running over a little old lady attempting to cross the street with a bag of groceries. She made a feeble effort to jump out of the way. Chico swerved widely, running a more nimble kid on a bike off the road, up onto the sidewalk. The kid yelled, "Slow down, hombre!"

Biff shifted nervously in his seat.

Chico observed his passenger's discomfort and commented, "No harm, no foul!"

He chuckled. Biff shook his head quietly in disapproval.

Carlos' directions proved accurate, especially in the case of the obscure dirt road turnoff to Sandoval's farm. Without specific directions, the turnoff would easily be missed.

"No wonder the authorities never found the drug runners in this remote hideout. Nothing conspicuous to alert anyone, appearing like hundreds of other farms in the remote, rural area," Biff mused, as Chico bounced the jeep down the bumpy, pot-holed lane to the farmhouse and barn."

Three miles later, they arrived at the farmhouse.

"Cozy arrangement," Biff observed the refurbished residence.

The place was a hubbub of investigative activity, with agents scurrying in every direction. Biff could see Serge and Carlos talking down the lane, as he climbed out of the SUV. They were huddled with the forensic team down by the old, weathered barn.

"Looks like the boys are on to something big, Chico," Biff observed. "Like hounds on the hunt!"

"Yes sir, Señor Roberts. They got the scent and are on the bad guys' trail. No stone left unturned", Chico replied as they walked towards the barn to join Serge.

"What's up Serge?" Biff enquired.

"Got four dead men here, under mysterious circumstances."

"We have no apparent clue as to their cause of their death!"

Serge came over close to Biff, whispering, "Don't know what happened. No sign of a struggle or foul play. This is fucking spooky!"

Serge wore a puzzled, frustrated expression, appropriate to the mysterious circumstances surrounding them.

"I only see two dead men by the barn door," Biff exclaimed.

"The other two are inside, face down in the hay along with three dead dogs and six rats!"

"Incredible!" Biff now interpreted Serge's look of astonishment, his frustrated demeanor.

"We have a forensic van with a pathologist on the way over from Cabo to haul the four cartel corpses back for autopsies and toxicology examinations. This is one weird fucking deal, let me tell ya, Biff."

"Got that right, Serge. I thought I'd seen everything. This is really bizarre."

Serge abruptly switched topics. He was animated, if not a bit rattled.

"Found the VW kidnapping van."

"Where?"

"Parked out back of the barn, rear window shattered. Retrieved your .9 mm bullet fragments."

"That ties Sandoval to the abduction." Biff interjected. "Where is he and the rest of the cartel?"

"They obviously cleared out in a hurry. Left the stove and coffee maker on. Probably around dawn, judging from all the lights they left on."

"Our source said the barn was the staging area for their contraband and the three Cuban canisters, but we've searched every inch with no evidence of either."

"Your source…?" Biff asked.

"Let's not visit that subject now, Biff. O. K.?"

Biff chose to let it go. A lot at stake here, his son, their mission, possibly national security, if the Langley intercepts were correct. They could have a philosophical discussion later.

"I assume they trucked everything out just before we arrived."

"Someone must have tipped them off," Biff suggested.

"I'm checking into that possibility."

"Where do you think they are heading?"

"La Paz. Our NSA intercepts suggest a northern sea rendezvous. There are only two roads out of here. One back southeast to Cabo, the other northeast to La Paz. They won't backtrack."

"Big news, Biff. We captured the 'fat man', Jorge Gomez, early this morning. He confessed a lot of valuable information. That's how we found this place off the beaten path."

"He did? Any leads to Boo?"

"In fact, he did indeed give us a credible lead to Boo, including linking the ransom note to Sandoval. He thinks your son, Boo, is 'safe and sound' in the hands of the local Catholic priest and the nuns at the only church in Todos Santos."

"Why aren't we on our way then to the church?"

"I was awaiting your arrival when we discovered this mess. It struck me as so extraordinary that I got bogged down, distracted. Actually, this crime scene blew my mind! I figured if Boo was at the church, he's safe, best to wait for you."

"Good judgment, Serge. You made the right call."

Biff could relate to Serge's explanation. Priorities change with the circumstances. This situation was unique in its challenge. Serge was doing his best, juggling priorities.

"Great news! Let's head for the church now, Serge."

Biff was beside himself with elation, excitement, and anticipation of a joyful reunion with his son. He couldn't wait to bring Boo back to Mary Beth. She'll go nuts that her prayers were answered.

"I sent one of my agents over to check the information out, when I got tied up here. Told him not to take any recovery action, just make some discreet enquiries. Make no waves. Let me call him for a current update, OK?"

"Hola, Antonio. Que pasa? What's happening? … Really… That's terrific news. We are on our way over."

"Antonio, I suspect Sandoval has posted a guard somewhere in the vicinity of the church. Go locate him now, and 'take him out to lunch'… You know what I mean, Antonio… It's just a fucking metaphor! … Look, let me make it crystal clear, kill the fucker! …Just don't create a lot of commotion, OK?" …

"I don't give a rat's ass how… Shoot him, stab him, strangle him… WTF's wrong with you? you dumb fuck!" Serge hung up, red in the face, neck veins bulging. He was really pissed!

Biff almost split his side laughing at Serge. He was a storybook character, larger than life. Serge lost it over the phone just now, much to Biff's amusement. Biff hadn't enjoyed such a good laugh since last Saturday's misfortune.

"Might have to kill the fucker myself, then shoot that dumb sumbitch agent I sent over there." Serge muttered, shook his head, and grinned sheepishly at Biff, who was still chuckling.

Serge cracked him up, "My God, he was funny."

"Sorry 'bout that, let's move out." Serge said with a smile, pleased that Biff was amused by his nasty, potty mouth tirade with that dumb ass agent. Serge did not suffer fools well.

Serge summoned two bodyguards, and headed to the consulate jeep. On the way, he contemplated Biff's amused reaction to his meltdown on the phone call to his subordinate, chewing him out with a stream of profanities.

Some uptight, 'politically correct' top dogs' in Biff's high position with the 'Company' would strenuously object to his phone remarks, definitely not PC, probably have his ass in a sling.

"Not Biff, he laughed his butt off. Look at him. He's still chuckling to himself five minutes later", Serge observed.

"That's the difference between an 'operative', and a Langley desk jockey," Serge concluded.

"Biff's gone through 'Hell and high water', and maintains his sense of humor and perspective under duress. Truly a remarkable man. Biff will make an exceptional CIA director someday," Serge predicted. "His reaction to my outburst is a leadership quality in short supply these days."

Biff was starting to experience a sense of relief, a huge weight off his shoulders. The family situation was improving fast. He'd soon be reunited with his son." Mary Beth will be ecstatic," he predicted.

Padre Miguel was praying when they arrived at the old Colonial Cathedral. Respectfully, they waited in the back, so as not to disturb him in his morning prayer of salvation.

The sanctuary's architecture displayed a certain charm with its high arched ceiling, common to old churches of this period. A bright ray of sunlight filtered through one of the stained glass windows, coming to rest on the good Padre's dark maroon robes and close cropped gray hair, as he knelt before the altar. It captured a reverent moment, moving both men who were secular in nature, not understanding the devotion required of a priest, but respecting his dedication. They patiently waited to speak with him.

Five minutes later, their patience was rewarded. The priest arose from the altar, and noticed the visitors, one a large, strong blond American.

"How may I help you gentlemen?" he cordially asked, surprised to see someone at this early hour on a Monday morning.

"Excuse me, Padre," Serge answered, showing deference to a man of the cloth.

"We need to ask you some important questions."

"This is Mr. Roberts from San Francisco. His son is missing, kidnapped last Saturday. We have reliable information indicating that the boy may be in your custody."

Padre Miguel eyed them suspiciously. His brother had told him the boy's father was abusive, becoming violent. This American did not fit this description in his initial impression. He decided to exercise caution, nevertheless.

"Should he shelter the boy from these men with some deception?" he debated.

"I'm sorry. Would you elucidate the circumstances involving the boy?"

The Padre was very composed, but hesitant and uncommitted.

Biff was becoming impatient, but he restrained himself from butting into the conversation. Let Serge manage it diplomatically. Mexico and its customs were his bailiwick. He would not let the good Father bamboozle him, if that was his intent. The Padre struck Biff as sincere, but wary. He was hiding something.

Serge continued politely, "Mr. Roberts is a visiting consultant at our consulate in Cabo San Lucas where I'm on the diplomatic staff."

Serge presented his credentials. Padre Miguel examined them closely, comparing the official passport photo to the man standing before him. He glanced back and forth. Once he confirmed Serge's identity, he returned the documents.

"Let me hear more, if you don't mind."

Maybe the boy's story was not delusional after all. Maybe he was not a 'runaway' from an abusive father as his brother, Ricardo, had presented the case. These men seemed genuine, their story quite convincing.

Perhaps Ricardo had deceived him for some ulterior motive. His brother could be 'sneaky' at times, although he had been a loyal and generous brother over the years. Why would he deceive me now? The boy had no physical evidence of abuse and responded normally to the nuns' care. He was well behaved. Something did not fit in the story. The priest was now confused.

Serge pressed on. "We've been searching for him since Saturday. Mr. Roberts received this ransom note." he handed the parchment letter to the Padre who closely examined it.

A mixed expression of confusion and astonishment came over the priest. He exclaimed, "My goodness! This is my church stationary, reserved for special occasions. The font is from my old typewriter in the church office."

He realized at this moment that Ricardo had lied to him about the boy, the circumstances, everything. He would pray for Ricardo's soul. He had strayed from God's path.

One more test to be certain. No need to compound his mistakes. The priest was slowly being persuaded by Serge's skillful presentation. Mr. Roberts had refrained from speaking. Why? Because the conversation switched frequently from English to Spanish? If he was searching for his son, I'd expect him to be more proactive. Maybe he just is overwhelmed with grief, completely dependent on his friend from the consulate to handle his personal matters, Father Miquel speculated.

"Mr. Roberts, may I ask you a few personal questions that only a father would know about his son." The priest asked in perfect English with an imperceptible accent.

"Wonder if he studied at an American seminary?" Biff mused.

"Would you describe the boy that you are looking for in detail?"

"Gladly, Padre." Biff glibly detailed Boo's distinctive characteristics in such detail that no one could doubt him. He even described the surfing trunks his son was wearing when kidnapped. And, Boo's signature cowlick and grin that he inherited from Biff. That cinched the deal with Padre Miguel.

"Come this way with me gentlemen," he smiled warmly as he led them to the hallway to the nunnery. "There has been a huge misunderstanding. Let me rectify it."

Boo was contently playing checkers with the nuns at the far end when they entered the comfy room, lined with bookcases, decorated in religious themes. Fresh cut flowers pleasantly scented the room, creating a warm atmosphere. A whiff of incense emanated from a small chapel adjacent to the room.

It was immediately evident that Boo had indeed been "in good hands", as Jorge Gomez had confessed.

Biff sighed in relief. "Thank you, Padre. Thanks, God!"

He ran to greet Boo who heard the commotion, jumped up, and ran to him. They met halfway and hugged.

"Dad, I knew you'd come find me!" he yelled with joy. "The nuns and Father Miguel prayed for you."

They continued hugging, Biff tussled his son's curly blond locks. No tears were shed.

"Good to see you, kid. Your mom and I really missed you!"

Serge and the Padre observed the joyous reunion. The priest had indeed prayed for Boo's 'abusive' father, as falsely portrayed by Ricardo.

The deception was over. Prayers had been answered. Father and son reunited, happily together again. A strong family bond reconstituted.

"Wait 'til your mother sees you, Boo. Let's go see her, OK?"

"Serge, I'll have Chico drive us back to Cabo Surf. I'll spend a couple of hours with Boo and his mom, then I'll hook up with you this afternoon, OK?"

"Sounds like a plan, Biff." Serge gave him and the Padre warm embrazos.

"Heading to La Paz, amigo."

CHAPTER TWENTY THREE
THE AUTOPSY — MONDAY 11 AM

"Biff, I'm tied up with 'business' here in La Paz. Checking all the marinas for 'fishing boats' for hired out recently. Autopsy summation is scheduled for 1pm. Will you cover me? Alicia has all the details and directions. Sorry to cut your family reunion short. Thanks, pal. Serge."

Biff understood the cryptic e-mail he just received on his coded Blackberry that Serge gave him to use. Of course he'd cover Serge, even though it meant less time with Boo and Mary Beth. The last two hours together as a family were the most happy moments in recent memory!

She was absolutely ecstatic to be reunited with their son and so proud of her husband. Biff came through again! Grateful that her prayers were answered, her faith became stronger than ever, Biff noticed. They planned a nice lunch together as a family reunion celebration. A champagne occasion.

Biff respected his wife's religious devotion. After the crisis that they had just been through, and the touching religious experience at the Catholic church earlier this morning, Biff wondered if his wife and Padre Miguel were onto something significant and sustainable,… religion.

"The experience may be life changing", he couldn't argue with the positive results in this case.

"Anecdotal," Biff assessed. "Not a scientific observation. But, how do you establish who is in the 'control group? Empirical evidence, I guess, that's why they call it 'religion.' It requires a leap of faith."

Biff was in a pensive, reflective mood. Not a 'come to Jesus' moment, but a brief, solemn reassessment of where he stood in mid-life, and what mindset would carry him forward. He felt like he'd just dodged a bullet, retrieving Boo. Recurrent life threatening events seemed a dramatic pattern in his CIA profession. He'd experienced several close calls in Vietnam, but this personal episode involving their son drained his deepest emotions. It called on his deepest reserves to sustain his rescue efforts. He recognized that without Serge's help, it would not have been accomplished.

His wife relied on her religion to sustain her. While Biff fell back on, well, himself. As an agnostic, he lacked a backup. If he failed, he failed. That is what drove him not to fail. Biff had no 'back up', no resource.

Religion and rendition remained on Biff's list of unresolved moral dilemmas. He had his inner conflicts. Basically, he viewed himself as a 'realist', his secular world view grounded in science, his philosophy attuned to existentialism.

Biff held himself accountable for his actions, 'Every day is judgment day', according to Caymus. Day to day, Biff took a simplistic, pragmatic approach to life, reducing problems to their common denominator. That always worked. This approach attained consistent results, well above average.

So, why should he change? His musings stopped abruptly.

"Honey, just received an e-mail from Serge. I've got to go back to the consulate. May get an answer to the' farm mystery' … A lot riding on this…Sorry."

"That's good that you may get an answer, dear. We're OK. Boo and I plan to hit the beach. His surfing experience was cut short. He told me that the 'surf's up'. I'd like to go home with a sun tan. I'll catch some rays, while he rides the waves", she said cheerfully.

"It's OK, Dad," Boo chimed in, "We'll see you tonight. Mom and I will have fun."

"Don't worry, Biff. We'll be OK. Still have our bodyguard."

She glanced in his direction, at the corner of the suite's balcony. He maintained a vigilant eye on them, never obtrusive, nor conspicuous.

"Sounds like you have a great day planned. Maybe I will join you for dinner, how's that sound?"

"We won't plan on it!" she laughed with her friendly jibe.

"She's back to normal," Biff observed. He went over and kissed her, and hugged Boo, tussling his hair playfully.

"See ya later. I love you guys!'

"I love you too, Biff. You always come through, dear!"

"Bye, Dad."

It was obvious that she had zero interest in his ongoing mission, even though she pretended. Naturally, her focus was her son. Actually, he was fully committed from here on out. Their vacation essentially was reaching its end. Surely, Mary Beth was inclined to return to San Francisco tomorrow with Boo.

"I'm tied up all week. You can stay here…" he said, as he started to leave.

"I've made reservations on tomorrow's flight to SF with Boo. You're so busy, and we are ready to get back home. I've had enough of Mexico for awhile, Biff. Trip was a bummer. Boo returns to prep school next week. We both need to unwind in familiar surroundings."

She made it easy for him, anticipating that he would suggest it.

"That's fine. I won't have much leisure time. I'm going to La Paz this afternoon. Maybe I'll make a late dinner, but probably won't be back for much family time."

She looked at him sadly. It was the story of her life. She said nothing to make him feel guilty.

Biff recognized the sadness in her eyes. He had second thoughts.

"So, in case I don't make dinner, why don't we have an early lunch on the veranda together?" The Consulate business can't wait for an hour. I've changed my mind."

He returned from the doorway and plopped on the sofa, stretching his legs on the coffee table.

He grinned, "Whata ya say, sweetheart?"

"You're on, big fella! Boo's just went in to brush his teeth. He will be delighted that you altered your plans to be with us awhile longer. As soon as he comes out, we'll head down to the veranda. It's such a lovely day!"

"In more ways than one," Biff commented.

She smiled, understanding full well the significance of his casual comment. He grinned widely in response. They connected.

Mary Beth was delighted that he abruptly changed his plans and did not rush off. A very uncharacteristic act for her husband. Finally, they would have some family time together, if only for an hour.

When the Roberts family showed up on the terrace for breakfast, the resort guests stood up, cheered loudly, and applauded them. The manager, Andres Delarosa heard the commotion, and came running out of his office. Viewing the crowds' jubilance, he ordered a round of mimosas for everyone. Pitchers full on each table. Time to celebrate!

The Roberts were appreciative, but embarrassed at the adulation shown them. Biff gave them a polite, brief salute, a signature grin, then sat down for the first family vacation meal together on this 'vacation' trip.

Halfway through breakfast, Chico, his consulate driver and bodyguard showed up, one half hour early. Seemed to be the story of his life lately.

"What's up, Chico?"

"Big wig from Washington, D.C. flying in. Everyone's hoping you can take Serge's post hosting him, since Serge is attending to business in La Paz. It's a hot potato, no one wants to deal with it Señor Roberts."

Biff kissed his wife goodbye, gave Boo a big hug, tussled his hair, and told him, "Take good care of your mom, big fellow."

"You bet, dad. See you in San Francisco, OK?" He hugged his father.

"Thanks for rescuing me, dad!"

"Not a problem, son. That's what daddy's do."

"Bye, sweetheart. Off again." He kissed her good bye.

"Why is he leaving in the middle of breakfast?" the morning diners wondered. "No let up for that guy! Some vacation…"

Off Biff went to the consulate. The autopsy was about to begin. Would the 'farm mystery' be solved? Who was the 'big wig'?

The CIA spared no expense to insure that the mystery would be solved, flying in three forensic experts from San Diego and L.A. on short notice, early that morning on a 'company' jet. Told that the autopsy mission was classified due to 'national security' concerns, the physicians signed a secrecy oath. The Mexican Consulate pathologist, Dr. Arandale was designated as the lead physician of the autopsy team.

The four forensic pathologists worked steadily and simultaneously, one each on the four cartel bodies. Early rigor mortis had set in. They knew of each other's reputation from journal articles and national meetings. They got along fine, working together as a team. The CIA had briefed them on the potential ramifications of the mysterious deaths. They were actually excited to do their part in unraveling the enigma.

The Doctors drew cardiac blood from each corpse for toxicology, drug panels, O&P, viral and bacterial cultures, plus routine smears for microscopic examination. They catheterized the dead men's bladders, sending urine samples for culture and sensitivity studies and routine urinalysis. No question, they were pro's at their job.

The Consulate pathologists were assisted by three local Mexican pathologists, flattered to be invited to participate in such a high profile case. Public relations at work.

There was no idle chatter. It was all serious business. All seven physicians took maximum precautions, wearing full length gowns, caps, masks, and double gloves. Whatever killed these drug traffickers would have to penetrate their protective cover. They'd take no chances.

Non-medical personnel were confined to the auditorium outside the glass windows of the pathology operating theater for their safety in case the 'cause of death' proved contagious. Whatever it was, it had already proved itself lethal.

Biff and Chico joined the gathering crowd awaiting the preliminary report. CIA personnel stood up in respect when Biff entered the small room. He grinned and signaled them to sit back down. The others present in the amphitheater wondered who the Hell this guy was, to command such respect?

The Doctors had been at it since 8 am, five hours ago. The corpses were laid open, stem to stern with median sternotomy and Rokatansky incisions exposing the internal organs in the chest and abdomen respectively. These huge incisions allowed gross examination of each organ and microscopic biopsy to determine the cause of death. The specialists were starting to formulate a differential diagnosis when Biff arrived.

No one present appreciated the enormity of the circumstances other than Biff. All were focused on the 'farm mystery', the cause of death of the four drug traffickers

Biff worried about a possible link to the NSA intercepts of Cuban messages, suggesting that a terrorist plot was brewing. Were the three Cuban canisters in Sandoval's cartel possession potentially part of a sinister scheme? The ramifications reached National Security levels.

A hush fell over the small gathering as Dr. Arandale, the chief pathologist emerged from the autopsy theater in fresh scrubs, leaving the contaminated clothing behind. He had a look of serious concern that he was about to share with the professional audience.

"At this point, we can conclusively report the cause of death in all four men to be" Bilateral Hemorrhagic Pneumonia", involving all lobes of each of the four men's lungs."

"The disease was as extensive as any ever witnessed by any of the seven examining physicians", he explained.

"To be present in all four victims to this severe extent, is an 'outlier' statistical observation, beyond two standard deviations.

"In layman's terms, 'highly unusual and unexpected, I'd say 'rare'. "

"In these four cases, it suggests exposure to an overwhelming dose of toxins or a highly virulent strain of bacteria or virus. Our findings suggest the men had been dead less than six hours. For all of them to die that quickly indicates or implicates an organism that releases a very powerful toxin that causes sepsis, a blood stream infection. This type of infection then overwhelms the victim, leading to vital systemic organ shutdown, and death."

"We are running additional tests at this time to confirm our hypothesis. Some tests take minutes, some days, but I anticipate that we soon will have our answer."

"We favor a bacterial etiology or cause with these particular Pneumonia findings. Gram stains for micro exam are underway. Should determine what killed them. We'll know in 10 or 15 minutes if our initial diagnosis is correct. Any questions?"

"Doc, how did all four men catch Pneumonia and die in 80 degree weather? They didn't even have cold symptoms, did they?" one of the detectives asked.

"I'd disregard the influence of temperature. Furthermore, we have no witness to report any prodromal signs or symptoms. The question is hypothetical."

The detective wished he hadn't asked the question.

Biff wondered, if he even understood the answer.

"Couldn't they have been poisoned? That would explain all of them dying at once, wouldn't it?" another enquired.

We considered that in our differential diagnosis, but ruled it out because it could not be correlated with our autopsy findings, unless it is some new agent not described in the literature causes a rapid, overwhelming hemorrhagic bronchopneumonia."

A lab technician suddenly came in through a side door, looking official in a long white coat. She interrupted him, handing him a lab report. The pathologist studied it closely. His expression changed to a grim frown.

"Gentlemen, we have our definitive answer to the mystery. 'Microscopic exam of the gram stain reveals:

GRAM POSITIVE ENCAPSULATED BACILLI
WITH NUMEROUS SPORES ON THE SLIDE
TYPICAL OF BACILLUS ANTHRACIS

"What the Hell does that mean, Doc?" A man in the front row asked.

"That means that if our lung tissue and blood cultures grow out these same lethal bacteria, these four men all died of septicemia associated with anthrax, a fatal bacterial infection. Once it invades the blood stream, it spreads its spores into vital organs, severely damaging them. Once the organs cease to function, the victim dies. In the case of anthrax, it happens very rapidly with large exposure."

"How'd they get Anthrax out on a farm in the middle of nowhere?" Carlos asked'

"Any sheep?" the doctor replied.

"SHEEP?" Carlos exclaimed, baffled. "Never saw one on the Baja Peninsula!"

"Not important in this case since the victims lacked cutaneous lesions associated with Woolsorters' Disease. Somehow, from some source, the victims inhaled a lethal dose of Anthrax bacteria and spores. The mechanisms remain unknown!"

"Once in the lungs, the bacilli's spores multiply like wildfire, releasing millions more bacteria into the blood stream leading to a fatal septicemia, as I mentioned earlier. I expect the blood cultures to verify this as the cause of death. I suspect confirmation in 24 hours or less."

Biff was seated near the middle of the room, listening to the exchanges and explanations, putting two and two together, thinking …

"Those three Cuban canisters must contain 'weapons grade' Anthrax, that somehow leaked out, killing all four cartel members. I'm the only one privy to the secret NSA intercepts. No one here is aware of this highly classified information…"

"Those seven doctors and lab techs have been exposed to deadly bacteria, despite their protective measures. I must warn them without divulging my sources and methods. They need prophylactic doses of Cipro!"

He stood up to address the chief pathologist. It was his solemn duty.

"Dr. Arandale, I'm Biff Roberts of the San Francisco Consulate. I can not reveal my source of information, but it is my moral obligation to warn you and your medical staff that in all probability, you have been exposed to highly lethal 'weapons grade' Anthrax. You and your staff should immediately start prophylactic treatment with the specific antibiotic of choice, Ciprofloxin. I'm not a doctor, but I know that Cipro is the advised course of action with certainty."

You could have heard a pin drop between audible gasps. All heads shifted to Biff, then back to Dr. Arandale at the podium, awaiting his response.

"Weapons grade'?" … the Doctor paused for clarification.

"By adding 1 to 2 % silicon to viable Anthrax spores, a lethal aerosol is formed. The silicon process requires a sophisticated lab, and know how. It is an extremely dangerous process."

Who said that? The statement came from the rear of the room, over by the door. Heads swung around to the back of the conference room.

All eyes looked back to focus on the owner of the deep, authoritative voice. Their eyes came to rest on a distinguished appearing, elderly gentleman peering down into the auditorium over his gold rimmed, granny spectacles, reminiscent of a college professor. The Harris Tweed jacket and foulard bow tie reinforced this impression. This man had presence, and projected authority. They eagerly listened to what he had to say next, hanging on every word.

"I suspect Mr. Roberts' assumption is correct. His recommendations regarding antibiotic certainly are absolutely the correct course of action. I'd urge immediate action."

Dr. Arandale quietly gave the order to an assistant.

"Good to see you again, Biff, even in these dire circumstances."

"Thank you for flying out from Fort Dietrich, Professor." Biff hastened to introduce the consultant.

"Gentlemen, this is Dr. Emil Alexander, a world renowned expert on Bioterrorism, especially 'weapons grade' anthrax. I cannot go into the details because of classified information, but, I warn that we may be facing an imminent terrorist threat. The autopsy results emphatically point in that direction."

"All of you are sworn to secrecy, you will sign an oath before you leave today. I'll let Dr. Alexander give you a run down on the dangerous implications. I'd like to request Dr. Arandale to order the Cipro regimen started, while Dr. Alexander briefs us. Please come on down to the podium, Professor."

The esteemed Professor established eye contact with the audience. He had their full attention.

"Since there are no witnesses, we must first assume these four men inhaled lethal doses of Anthrax. The autopsy results confirm that."

"Secondly, we must assume an aerosol form of the spore was present. Nothing less would have killed them that quickly."

"A third assumption is tenuous, a hypothetical. The cartel must have been storing the lethal bacteria in the barn and the container leaked or was tampered with."

"Without going into sensitive Intel. details, a fourth assumption postulates a collusion of the cartel with a foreign government intent upon attacking the USA. The cartel facilitates the transfer of the terrorists' Anthrax, but an accident occurs, infecting these four men, killing them in an alarmingly short period of time."

"All four scenarios are plausible explanations. Let me present a brief overview of the infectious disease process, so you can better understand the current situation."

"Three factors influence the outcome, life or death."

"The offending organism's virulence, and exposure dose have a linear relationship. Simply put, the more virulent the bacteria and the higher the dose, the greater the lethality, the quicker the victim dies."

"Conversely, host resistance may confer immunity in many infectious diseases. Unfortunately, no one is immune to a deadly Anthrax exposure. There is no host resistance."

The audience listened intently. The tech in the long white lab coat returned with a large box of Cipro, which she started dispensing to the six Pathologists and tech's who had joined Dr. Arandale in seats next to him to hear the visitor's lecture.

Biff quietly observed the professionalism of this group after just hearing the staggering news that they may die, if they fail to take the Cipro. They complied, taking the antibiotic without further discussion.

"Even with a small initial dose, the spores can multiply in the lungs rapidly. A fraction, a few grams of inhaled Bacillus may contain 5000 to 8000 spores, sufficient to cause a serious lung infection."

Biff thought, "That should reassure the Pathologists…"

"….Once the spores gain a foothold, fatal septicemia with multi organ failure is inevitable without antibiotic intervention." The professor continued.

"The process of fermenting and adding silicon to the Bacillus spores is a tedious, complicated, and dangerous task, as we know from firsthand experience at our Fort Dietrich lab. I suspect that this batch probably came from Iraq or Iran. I'll have one of my techs fly out to identify the markers. After Baghdad fell, our intel teams discovered 8500 liters of 'weapons grade' Anthrax in Iraq, a little known fact. In the wrong hands, Anthrax is a devastating bioterrorist 'weapon of mass destruction.'"

"Everyone focused only on Iraqi nuclear threats, and neglected to mention this alarming discovery in all the hubbub about, 'no weapons of mass destruction were found,' a political statement. Iraq also harbored a large store of 'mustard gas', an outlawed WW 1 nightmare!"

Audible sighs swept through the amphitheater. This was astounding news!

"Not finding something, does not rule out its existence!"

"Bioterrorism is frightening. A small amount of weapons grade anthrax can reap havoc! It is difficult to counter. Next to a 'dirty bomb', it produces the maximum psychological impact that the terrorists strive for in their warped minds, and nefarious plots."

Biff was already texting Langley,

'Standby for secure back channel communication, TOP PRIORITY.'

CHAPTER TWENTY FOUR

US CONSULATE CABO
SAN LUCAS – MONDAY PM

Following the autopsy, Biff hustled over to Serge's office. Alicia greeted him,

"Buenas tardes, Señor Roberts."

"Good afternoon, Alicia. I need a secure back channel line to Langley immediately. See if you can locate Serge in La Paz. I need to speak with him, as soon as I complete my urgent call back East."

"Si, Señor."

She led him to Serge's back office and unlocked the door to the small high tech room equipped with cutting edge electronic communication paraphernalia. She politely pointed out a high speed auto dial system that Serge had installed. Organized alphabetically by country, it was possible to contact any embassy or consulate CIA operative under diplomatic cover by simply pressing the proper speed dial button. The room was sound proof with the door closed.

"Nice set up, Alicia."

Alicia pointed out the "USA – Langley" button. She assured him the line was secure. A technician checked it for bugs daily.

"I'll go track down Serge. Call me if you need help, Señor Roberts."

"This will not take long, Alicia. Thank you for your assistance.

"Jim, Biff Roberts calling. Got a tiger by the tail! Autopsies turned up Anthrax!"

"No, I'm not kidding ... Emil Alexander is convinced that it's 'weapons grade'... you heard me right... 'weapons grade!'... Emil said that is the only rational explanation for all four bad guys dying that quickly with overwhelming inhalation hemorrhagic bronchopneumonia!... Agree, he's the expert... got to go with his recommendations... I concur; the NSA intercepts were right on ... Had to be the Cuban canisters... Agree... Yeah... OK... You got it, Jim... That is the essence of the 'barn mystery', how'd the canister leak without killing everyone?... Right ... OK, you will take it from here... All security agencies on high alert... 'four alarm fire' code... You got it, Jim. Over and out."

Biff locked the door and returned the key to Alicia.

"Serge said to use his office phone and call him in five minutes at this number."

She handed Biff the La Paz Phone number that she'd jotted down on her note pad. He placed the call on Serge' private line. Serge answered immediately.

"No fucking way! Weapons grade Anthrax killed all four cartel dudes? Right out of a sci-fi movie. Unreal! So, that's what is in the Cuban containers. Strikes me as a scary proposition, transporting those canisters, Biff. What's to prevent another accidental leak, killing a crowd?" Serge asked.

"Who knows? Anthrax is the key to the puzzle, the 'barn mystery.'"

"Tell me more, Biff. This caper is blowing me away"

"Got to go with the opinion of the world expert from our weapons lab in Fort Dietrich. Dr. Emil Alexander presented a very convincing case that an aerosol preparation of concentrated Anthrax spores is the only reasonable explanation for the severity of the inhalation hemorrhagic pneumonia that killed all four of the men so rapidly."

"So, who would have suspected that those steel canisters that the Cubans are transporting contained 'weapons grade' Anthrax! But, Biff, how did the lethal bacteria get out of those canisters without killing everybody, not just those four bad guys?"

"That, my good man, is the unresolved part of the 'barn mystery.' Serge, no one can explain it. The professor treats it as a mute point. Lacking material evidence, you rely on deductive reasoning. The four dead men had identical findings at autopsy, irrefutable evidence of Anthrax bacilli and spores in their diseased lungs, the 'worst' the pathologists had 'ever seen', as Dr. Arandale described it.'"

"Emil attributed these observations to the inhalation of siliconized bacilli spores dispersed in the barn air, leading rapidly to the bad guy's demise."

"Sumbitch! This is unreal, Biff. We have to intercept those Cuban canisters before they reach the States."

"Absolutely, Serge. That is the game plan. Discover any leads up there?"

"Checked the usual haunts, the usual suspects. Got the Federales involved showing our artist's sketch of Sandoval? No one would forget seeing him! So far, no leads."

"Sandoval's clever. He may avoid the usual hideouts. Better think outside the box, Serge."

"Good point, I'll check the local Christian Science reading room."

Both men laughed at Serge' wry humor.

"Found what we think is their farm truck in one of the marina's parking lots. Checked with the marina commodore who said he saw nothing unusual today, just a steady stream of fishermen, mostly tourists.

I described Sandoval to him, showed him the sketch. He laughed. Said a guy that strange would have caused a ruckus among the locals. They take their fishing seriously up here in La Paz. Don't want oddballs hanging around."

"Did you check out the farm truck?"

"Thought you'd never ask."

"Don't tell me it belongs to Sandoval."

"Baja plates from Todos Santos are registered to none other than Jorge Gomez. How's that grab you?"

"Interesting, very interesting, Serge."

"Searched the truck top to bottom, found nothing. Nada. So I borrowed a 'Sniffer' dog from the local sheriff. Put him on the flatbed. The dog went nuts! Sheriff says his dog never misses weed or coke."

"That tells me they off loaded the contraband at the dock, boarded a boat, and are headed North."

"Better redeploy the Coast Guard, Serge."

"Already done, Biff. I don't think the truck was left there as a decoy. Sandoval and the Cubans are at sea."

"What next?" Biff asked.

"I've got agents posted in the marina to question all returning boat crews. Someone should identify Sandoval and his drop off point. I suspect they switched to a more seaworthy craft offshore for the long journey up to the Gulf of California. Once they identify this craft, the Coast Guard or spotter planes or choppers will intercept Sandoval and the Cubans."

"Sounds like a good plan, Serge. Shall I come up there to meet you?"

"I have some unfinished business to attend to at the Consulate. I'm on my way back. I'd suggest that you check on your family, pack a bag and your toothbrush, because we are going on a long journey."

CHAPTER TWENTY FIVE
THE CONFRONTATION – LATE MONDAY

S erge had pondered the distinct possibility of a 'mole' in a critical position at the consulate. He had to come to grips with the problem.

Gomez' interrogation implicated someone with access to classified information. That narrowed it down to six. He could not deny that someone privy to classified communications tipped Ricardo Sandoval on a timely basis.

Coincidence would be a rationalization as an explanation. Sandoval made clever moves to elude them, but Serge now realized he was getting inside information on a regular basis, facilitating his 'clever getaways.' That explained a lot of things.

Biff's premonition became reality when Jorge Gomez confirmed during his interrogation that 'an informant' occupied a high position at the Consulate.

It was time to take care of some unfinished business, no matter how unpleasant.

Serge had narrowed the list of suspects from six down to two 'trusted' employees with access to classified information. After he discovered that Biff's itinerary, wired over secure channels days before his arrival last

Friday evening had been 'intercepted', and not reported to him, Serge narrowed his suspicion to one person.

He did not want to believe it, but he concluded that he must confront that person and put the issue to rest. It would be painful, but it required resolution. The Consulate's CIA clandestine mission status had been compromised. It was time to take action.

Serge hit the intercom button.

"Alicia, would you come into my office, please." His voice had an edge of irritation to it, surprising Alicia.

Alicia picked up on his tone. "What's bugging him?" she wondered.

"Yes sir, I'll be right there."

She entered with her characteristic smile and pleasant carriage.

"Please sit down, Alicia." He said sternly.

Alicia did as told, sensing something serious was about to transpire.

Serge came right to the point, speaking harshly.

"Alicia, it has come to my attention that we have a 'mole' in our Consulate."

"A 'mole'?" She was unfamiliar with the term. Was he complaining about some rodent?

"A spy ", he clarified, recognizing the she didn't know the jargon.

"A spy? she asked somewhat coyly.

"Yes, Alicia, a spy. And, unfortunately all the evidence points to you!

Stunned by the accusation, she almost fell off her seat.

"What are you saying, sir?"

Serge went into his 'hard ass 'mode, not because he was angry, but because he felt betrayed by someone he considered beyond reproach.

"Alicia, I suspect you are the 'mole', the spy." he put it bluntly.

"You can confess and we will go lightly on your jail sentence."

"Jail?" This was not going well!

"Or, I'll turn you over to the contractors and let them extract a confession from you. It's your choice."

"Contractors?" she asked fearfully, starting to tremble.

"Jail would be the wiser choice", she quickly concluded." She was familiar with the contractors' reputation. She feared torture far more than time in a grubby Mexican jail.

"It's your choice, Alicia," Serge grimly pronounced, impatiently awaiting her decision, tapping his desk top like a metronome.

Alicia tried to buy time, like a trapped animal looking for a way out of a maze of trouble, not knowing which path to take.

"What do you imply, Señor Betancourt?" hedging…

"I've been a loyal employee to you… " a last ditch effort.

"I'm not implying anything, Alicia. I'm flat out accusing you of being a sneaky little spy, informing Ricardo Sandoval of our every plan. He knows our intentions, our planned moves, so he always has a 'heads up', allowing him to stay a step ahead of us, eluding the authorities, escaping just in the nick of time!"

Serge lashed out at her, showing his rare mean side, Alicia started crying, covering her face with her hands. Mascara ran down her cheeks, while Serge continued to berate her.

"I've paid you well. Treated you well. Why on Heaven's earth would you betray me? My staff? The U.S. Consulate?"

His tirade continued. Serge was red in the face, his neck veins bulging. He was really pissed! Dressing her down.

"Why, Alicia? Please tell me, why? I find it difficult to believe you would commit such criminal acts!"

This confrontation was painful for Serge, although his aggressive behavior belied it. He liked Alicia like the daughter he hadn't seen or heard from in years. It grieved him to confront her in this manner, but it was his sworn duty. He had to do it.

Serge' perception missed the reality of Alicia's personal situation. She was in a really tight spot, 'damned if I do, damned if I don't!'

Out of frustration, Serge asked her one more time.

"For God's sake, Alicia, why did you do it?"

Alicia sunk back in her seat, sobbing. Pale, nervous, upset. Tears filled her lovely, dark eyes. Her life torn between loyalty to two vastly different men, worlds apart. She loved them both. She must confess.

"Señor Betancourt, Ricardo Sandoval is my father!"

CHAPTER TWENTY SIX
CIA HEADQUARTERS, LANGLEY VA - TUESDAY 6 PM

"Gentlemen, we are facing a National emergency, an imminent bio-terrorist threat! It is a credible threat involving 'weapons grade' Anthrax.

A hush fell on the CIA conference room. The director had just dropped a 'bombshell' for starters. No one knew why the Director had called an emergency meeting at dawn until his dramatic opening statement.

"NSA intercepts indicated that an intricate Cuban plot was brewing almost one year ago. About two weeks ago, a 'special' shipment left Santiago Naval Base bound for Mexico. The plot intensified at that point."

"Coincidentally, two of our most experienced operatives, both well known to you, were in Baja Mexico investigating a cartel trafficking in drugs and weapons, a new twist in that illicit business, by the way."

"While Roberts and Betancourt were tracking this cartel, credible evidence surfaced tying this cartel to two Cuban terrorists transporting three steel canisters, presumably the 'special' shipment. Talk about an ironic twist of fate in our favor!"

"The basic plan, it appears, involves Cuba contracting with this experienced cartel to escort their two commandoes with their deadly cargo over established desert smuggling routes into the one of the Southwestern states to commit an act of terrorism."

Everyone in the audience listened intently to this story of international intrigue. The Director laid it all out concisely. He was a pro at summation.

"As our field officers closed in on the drug ring at a remote Baja farm, they found four dead cartel members in the farm's barn, without an apparent cause of death. Cognizant of the NSA intercepts, they wisely organized forensic autopsies and flew in Dr. Emil Alexander from our Bioterrorism lab in Maryland for expert consultation."

"Let me digress for a moment, gentlemen. This is a classic example of experienced field officers exercising good judgment and taking the initiative without concern to cover their asses. They took decisive action without dicking around with a lot of bureaucratic BS. This is an objective that we strive to engender here at Langley and our training center at the farm. The CIA strive to ingrain positive instinctive behavior. Obviously, we succeeded in the case of these two commendable field operatives. Consider this a teachable moment, gentlemen."

"OK, here's the nitty gritty, people. The post mortem studies documented the bad guys died of 'Bilateral Hemorrhagic Pneumonia associated with Anthrax bacteria and spores.'"

"Dr. Alexander concluded that the only rational explanation for these autopsy findings was inhalation of concentrated spores in a silicon aerosol. In other words, 'weapons grade' Anthrax, a formable bioterrorism tool, capable of killing thousands in a short period of time."

"The CIA will take the lead in coordinating "Operation Road Runner", an interagency counter-terrorism measure to avert this threat to our homeland."

The staff officers listened intently, taking notes.

"This operation will involve a concerted effort by all domestic security agencies. Homeland Security has authorized six drones to patrol the SW deserts, concentrating on the usual smuggling routes. The Border Patrol is stepping up their sweeps along the 'weak' entry points where the border fence has not been constructed. The DEA and FBI will collaborate with us, sharing intelligence, both Humint and electronic information. Our command post is being set up at Luke AFB in Phoenix, as we speak."

"Presently, we are concentrating our efforts to intercept the terrorists before they reach our soil. The Mexican government has been extremely cooperative and helpful. The current focus is the Sea of Cortez and Gulf of California with air and sea surveillance. The Mexican Coast Guard are boarding ships and boats unannounced. The Federales are scouring all the ports along the Gulf's route north."

"I need you gentlemen to summon all your acumen and experience to thwart this potential threat. We must avoid another 9/11! Let's spend the next few hours barnstorming, sorting through any conceivable scenario, no matter how far out. Hopefully, we'll come up a solid game plan. The cost of averting a potential disaster will be enormous. But the cost of life and damage by failing to prevent a bioterrorist attack is unthinkable!"

CHAPTER TWENTY SEVEN
THE CHASE – LA PAZ – LATE
MONDAY AFTERNOON

"You are not going to believe this, Biff."

"How's that, Serge?" Biff settled into the suite's sofa to receive the phone call. Serge could get loquacious, might as well get comfortable. He was awaiting Serge's call to coordinate their trip to La Paz. Serge had returned to town to 'take care of some 'unfinished business'.

"I discovered the mole in our Consulate. Your premonition was spot on…"

"Really? That's great news. How'd you do it?"

Serge's opening announcement caught his full attention.

"In one of the most difficult confrontations of my life…"

"First, I finally figured out how Ricardo Sandoval stayed one step ahead of us. We just missed nabbing him yesterday at the farm, and at the marina in La Paz this morning. He's a clever fox, I credit him, but much of his success can be attributed to 'tip offs', coming directly from an in- house informant. Someone privy in my inner circle. I came up with a list of suspects."

"Then I weaned this list of six suspects, who had access to classified information, down to the only person who could possibly have known your Mexico itinerary and not purposely informed me last week. Finally, I confronted that suspect with my accusations."

"It was ugly and painful, Biff."

"And…the suspense is killing me, Serge. Come to the point please. Who is the mole?"

"The mole is Alicia Nicascio! My sweet little secretary. Can you fuckin' believe that?"

"What?! She would definitely not have been high on my list of possible informants. She really doesn't fit the picture of a spy. She sure fooled me!"

"A missed perception. My antenna didn't receive that subliminal signal", Biff reflected.

"I'm usually a good judge of people. Dammit! Sorry to hear that, Serge."

"How 'bout me? Worked for me for over six years, since she was 18 y.o. She was like family to me. But, it gets worse, Biff."

"How could it possibly get worse?"

"I asked her why she betrayed me and the Consulate to help a cartel jefe escape capture? We had treated her royally. Paid her well. Her covert actions just didn't make sense. What in the Hell did she have to gain? What motive? It was just crazy, unexplainable behavior on her part!"

"What did she say?"

"Her answer hit me like a brick! Blew me away! Incredible! As I said, you will not believe it!…"

"Alicia confessed that she was the illegitimate daughter of Ricardo Sandoval!"

"You are putting me on, Serge. This is not a joking matter. Get serious…"

Biff never knew what direction Serge's sense of humor would take. He came up with some off the wall stuff. Sometimes, Serge came across as 'unpredictably crazy'.

"Not kidding, pal. Listen to this story. I could not make this up. It'll knock your socks off."

"Her mother died in a terrible car accident, hit by a drunk, when Alicia was 15 years old. Alicia never lived with or even knew her father until then. Her mother never mentioned him."

"The day after the tragedy, Sandoval shows up, out of the blue. Handles the funeral. Tells Alicia that he is her father, explains the entire circumstances. He kindly arranges for someone trustworthy to care for her, since he's coming and going, doesn't have the time. He buys her a cozy apartment in a nice part of town, a couple of blocks from the beach. Considerately, he pays for years to send her to a private Catholic school. Daddy then regularly deposits six K a month in her account at Banamex. Believe me, he takes good care of her. Well educated and efficient, she earns three K at the Consulate. That's nine K a month, serious money down here, Biff."

"Good money anywhere, Serge. At least Sandoval is not a complete scoundrel. That's a glimpse into another side of a villain's personality. May be a little good in all of us," Biff offered.

Biff reflected a moment, philosophically, amazed at this human interest story. He realized how difficult it must have been for Serge to confront someone he had so trusted and respected, who deceived him, betrayed him.

"'Honor among thieves' thing, Biff. This whole episode is mindboggling. Alicia told me he avoids being seen with her to protect her reputation, but makes every effort to assure that she is well provided for. Even tells her how much he loves her. Sends her flowers on her birthday and holidays."

"Tough situation to deal with, Serge. She told you all of this personal information? Why?"

"She told me I was like a second father to her. That she was conflicted between two loyalties. Crushed me!"

After a long pause…in which each was at a rare loss for words…

"Now that you've got that trying emotional episode behind you, we can concentrate on heading off Sandoval and the Cuban canisters. What's the present status in La Paz?"

"Carlos is up there combing the docks. A lot of the boats didn't return until almost midnight. Some haven't returned yet. Fishing was 'gangbusters' out by the offshore islands. Boats staying out longer. He and the agents are interviewing every single captain regarding transporting Sandoval, the two Cubans, and the three cartel members. Our artist's sketch of Ricardo has been valuable. No one would confuse him with the Lone Ranger!"

Biff laughed at Serge' choice of comparison. Serge was on Biff's short list of unforgettable characters.

"I was about to leave my office to pick you up for our journey, but I have to wrap up the legal matters at the Consulate. I sure did not expect this complication with Alicia. So, I'm postponing our trip. Sorry. We'll head up to La Paz early in the morning. Gives you some more family time, OK?"

"Works for me. Wife's ecstatic to have Boo back."

"Packed your bag? We aren't coming back 'til we catch 'em!"

"Ready to go, amigo. Packed a small duffel. Wife and Boo are taking my suitcase with them tomorrow morning. Chico's driving them to the airport."

"OK. Pick you up in the morning, around 8. Little over a two hour drive to La Paz. We have a few hours of daylight left. Go take a swim in the ocean and relax with your family. See ya soon."

"Mary Beth, I've got a reprieve. Let's go for a swim. Grab, Boo. I wondered what the sea was like down here."

"Tell me you are not kidding, Biff."

"No way! I'm spending the night." He grinned widely. His wife ran to hug him.

The next morning, Serge and his bodyguards picked Biff up at ten am, allowing him to have an early breakfast with his family, and see them off to the airport.

They arrived at the La Paz municipal marina by late Tuesday morning, immediately spotting Carlos chatting with the Commodore on the dock. He waved, smiled, and gave a 'thumbs up' sign as they approached, indicating a positive break in the chase.

After exchanging the customary greetings, Carlos broke the news.

"Talked to the Captain who ferried Sandoval's group out to Isla Espirito Santo yesterday. Paid top dollar. Said Sandoval and the Cubans kicked back on the beach all day in the shade of the palm trees, drinking beer. The Captain and the others Rooster fished until nightfall. 'Knocked them dead,' he said. 'Never experienced better surf trolling.'"

"How far out is Espirito Santo? Sorry to interrupt," Serge enquired.

Carlos was heavy into fishing, Biff observed.

"About 14 or 15 miles NE, boss. Anyways… the bad guys BBQ 'ed some fresh Dorado on the beach, drank some more beer, then about ten o'clock, Sandoval requested the captain to drop the six of them and their Zodiac off at Isla Partida."

"Ísla Partida?"… Serge asked.

"A smaller island about 4 or 5 miles north of Espirito Santos, 20 to 25 miles NE from here. The captain said Sandoval even had the GPS coordinates written down for him."

"Any reason given?"

"Sandoval said he had an important rendezvous at midnight. But, if he told the captain the details, he'd have to kill him! Then he laughed like a madman."

"The captain said he thought Sandoval had too much beer aboard, but didn't want to cross this sinister looking dude. Didn't dare test him."

"So, he took them up and dropped them off on Partida just after 11 pm. They went ashore in their Zodiac. Once they were safely ashore, after the second Zodiac trip back and forth from his boat, the captain headed back the harbor."

"The 'second trip' bit, I didn't get it."

"Captain said they had a lot of packages, bundled in heavy plastic, probably coke and pot. Plus, the captain mentioned that the Cubans carried three green, steel containers which they never let out of their sight. Watched them like a hawk. It took two trips to get all this stuff ashore."

"Did the captain spy any sea craft waiting to pick them up?"

"Said the remote island was deserted, didn't see anything, and nothing for miles showed on his radar. For all he knows they may still be sitting there, waiting."

"I doubt that, but we'll get a surveillance helicopter to fly over to check it out. They have a 10 to 12 hour head start on us. Knowing their departure point may help the Coast Guard target their direction and cut them off."

"The Coast Guard have already boarded over 500 vessels in the general area. Pissed off a lot of fishermen who don't give a rat's ass about intercepting Cuban terrorists." Carlos reported.

"What's your best bet, Serge? What destination best suits their scheme? Maybe we can leapfrog them."

"Let me think. They need a small northern town not too far from the border to cross the desert into the States. Let's look over this nautical map the Commodore gave me. Every harbor along the gulf is detailed."

The two operatives studied the map. Biff pointed out a town located on the NE tip of the sea, not too far from California or Arizona, depending on which remote desert one chose to hazard across.

Serge looked closely, weighing the possibilities… "Yeah. If I was a drug trafficker, I'd probably land here."

"Point Penesco, or Rocky Point, as the Americans call it. A little resort town, not much bigger than a typical Mexican fishing village. Visited there several years ago on a fishing trip. Sandy beaches, not many reefs, the chart indicates. Looks like a safe harbor to land a Zodiac at night. After the bars close at 2 am, they roll up the streets and sack out. That would be my best bet, Biff. Better head on up. It's an educated guess. We've dispatched Federales to every northern port. They will be on the lookout for these dudes. We should be able to cut 'em off."

"I certainly hope so, Serge."

"One problem."

"What's that, Serge?"

"No airport. It's on the eastern side of the sea. No boat is fast enough for us to overtake them."

"That's no problem. We'll hire a seaplane."

"Who will fly it, if we find one?"

"A Mexican pilot, or me." Biff stated emphatically."

"Yeah, right." Serge scoffed. Sometimes Biff gets carried away. Thinks he is '007'. He challenged him.

"Where did you learn to fly a seaplane?"

"Alaska, looking for Russian spies in the outback and tundra, but that's a long story for another time." Biff shot back, grinning, sensing Serge was tweaking him.

Biff checked with the marina office. A sightseeing business operated out of a separate port about one quarter of a mile south along the beach path, an easy walk. Off they went.

Locating the office, they entered to enquire about hiring a flight to Rocky Point. Colorful posters advertised the "Beautiful Outer Island tours." It was a small operation, the pilot and a young deck hand for docking assistance.

Biff spoke to them in fluent Spanish.

Turned out the pilot could not fly them to Rocky Point today. His wife was expecting to deliver their third child this afternoon, he was committed to be at the hospital. "Sorry."

Two thousand dollars cash couldn't change his mind.

"How about if I rent it and fly it? I'll leave my American Express card with you as security."

The Mexican pilot just laughed, thinking this gringo was putting him on. He could not be serious, no way!

"How do I know you can fly, amigo?"

"Test me, hombre."

"OK, let's see what you've got."

He knew he could fly his plane from the copilot's right seat, so there was essentially no risk to him or his seaplane. He was up to Biff's proposition. This was 'a first' in his experience.

"These American's are 'loco'," he thought.

Serge observes this exchange and watches them climb into the six seat, Beaver seaplane.

Biff started the engine, and casually taxied out of the seaport, heading the Beaver upwind. He gunned the engine with a roar. With a powerful thrust they were soon air born.

"I'll be damned!" Serge uttered. "That guy is unreal!"

Twenty minutes later Biff executed a perfect landing, nose up slightly. The Beaver's pontoons splashed onto the calm surface., creating a wake as he taxied. The wake bounced boats against their moorings. Bait fish jumped out of the wake. Seagulls took flight at the disturbance. One experienced albatross remained, selecting his meal, fish jumping in the seaplane's ripples.

Successfully docking, out they climbed, Biff grinning, the pilot laughing.

"Some kinda gringo!" He slapped Biff on his back in a friendly fashion, laughing at this experiience.

Biff settled the business, filed a VRS flight plan, and they were airborne twenty minutes later. The flying conditions were perfect.

Serge had dispatched two commando teams in speed boats six hours earlier. He contacted them over the Beaver's radio system.

"'Roadrunner' departed Isla Partida around midnight, presumably heading NE. Possible destination Punta Penesco. Sea craft ID unknown. Be on alert. Coordinate activity with Mexican Coast Guard at sea, and Federales on shore. Over and out."

CHAPTER TWENTY EIGHT
NSA HEADQUARTERS — LANGLEY, VA. WEDNESDAY

"Hey, Chief. Take a look at these satellite photos that just came in. Pretty interesting."

Henry Lancaster, the senior Naval NSA officer on duty sauntered over to Lt. Andrews' desk, curious to see what he was so excited about.

He closely examined the photos laid out on the desk.

"Hmm... looks like a sub, an old Russian model. It's a night satellite photo sequence, images not all that clear with the heavy cloud cover."

"Where was this sighted, Lt.?"

"Check out the coordinates, bottom left, Chief", the NSA tech engineer politely replied. His Chief was a bit slow on the uptake this morning. Looked tired. The bioterrorist alert kept senior officers on duty, a 'wartime' exercise. This was the naval branch at the National Security Agency.

The senior CIA intelligence officer carefully studied the photos.

"Coordinates : Latitude – 31° 19'00" N

Longitude – 113° 32'13" W"

"I'm not familiar with these coordinates, Lt., exactly where is this sub?"

"I checked it out, Chief. The sub is located at the northeastern edge of the Gulf of California, about 150 Km from our SW border. There is a small fishing town near there, Puerto Penasco. Americans vacation there. Close to Arizona and California, They call it 'Rocky Point' ."

"The town is located on a relatively narrow strip of land in the state of Sonora that joins the Baja peninsula with the mainland of Mexico"

"Ahh…now I get it. The apex of the Sea of Cortez where Baja meets the mainland. I see you did your homework, Lt. Good job. Well done."

"You know, son, I should have known that. 'Expect the unexpected', an old NSA 'proverb.' So, we have an old Russian submarine in Mexican waters. Of course, … quite obvious. How'd I miss that?" He joked at his own expense.

Both men chuckled at his good natured humor.

"OK, Lt. What in the Hell is a Russian sub doing in remote Mexican waters in the middle of the night?

"I suspect the sub ties in with 'Operation Roadrunner', Chief. The Cabo caper involving Cuban bioterrorists."

Henry Lancaster realized this sharp, young Lt. was one step ahead of him today.

"By God! I think you are correct, Lt. That fits! You are on the ball today."

"Thank you, Sir."

"Those clever bastards transported the 'weapons grade' Anthrax and the bioterrorists under the sea's surface, explaining why the Coast Guard failed to intercept them. What an ingenuous scheme!"

"Notify command post and copy all security agencies stat on the emergency line. Get word and copies of the photos to our field officers, Roberts and Betancourt who are coordinating the Mexican aspect of 'Roadrunner'"

"Yes sir, right away, Sir."

As the bright young Lt. rushed off to obey his command, Admiral Lancaster thought,

"Lt. Andrews comes up for review next month. I'll see that he is promoted to commander, jumping a grade. The service needs outstanding young officers in decision making positions. Andrews has the qualifications. He merits a big promotion if his alertness this morning helps avert a National disaster."

CHAPTER TWENTY NINE
PUERTO PENASCO, MEXICO — THURSDAY AM

"**S**erge, look at these satellite photos that NSA forwarded."

Biff was fixated on his laptop computer screen in the only WI-FI spot in town, Starbucks. It was 6 am. Over java and pastries they were commiserating that Sandoval and the Cubans with their deadly canisters had apparently slipped through their sea and land traps. The big question, did they safely land here and rendezvous with a coyote?

Despite Federales in all northern ports and potential landfalls, and a net of Coast Guard fleet ships and boats, plus spotter planes' and helicopters' widespread surveillance of the Baja gulf, Sandoval had cleverly eluded them once again, a virtual Houdini.

"This photo might explain our failure to head them off, Serge."

A look of amazement came over Serge' face as he leaned over Biff's shoulder, studying the computer's screen.

"A submarine! WTF! How the Hell did they come up with that? Sumbitch! No wonder we couldn't find those bastards!"

It was early. Not many customers were present in Starbucks. But, the half dozen early birds seeking a caffeine jolt, all looked up at Serge' outburst of profanities, their expressions questioning, "What's your problem, buddy?"

Biff turned in their direction, grinned and announced, "Sorry, guys. My buddy's excitable. I'll get him to control his 'potty mouth,' OK?" He nudged Serge, "Easy, big fella!"

"Sorry, guys!". Serge turned and apologized, a seminal event for him.

They studied the screen together," Looks like an old sub," Serge offered his opinion. Biff followed with his.

"It's a '79 Soviet Kilo class diesel-electronic submarine. Very effective for coastal missions, like this, where high speed and long range are not crucial." Biff rattled off the sub stats like he was conducting a seminar.

"Surface speed of 12 knots, submerged, the sub will clip along at 16 knots. Actually, faster and quieter than a nuclear sub. Capable of escaping sonar detection under water when running on electronic motors, virtually silent."

"How do you know all this, Biff?" Serge asked, impressed with Biff's encyclopedic knowledge of an esoteric topic, 'soviet subs.'

"Read a lot of Tom Clancy techno-thrillers, Serge", he joked.

"Seriously, I rotated through the Naval War College during a required post-grad training session. At my pay grade, I attend a lot of courses."

"Gotta know your enemy's weapon capability, play 'war games.'"

"Hey, hombre, you're up to speed. I'm impressed."

Biff just grinned, then laughed, "It's called 'one ups man ship', pal"

"That sub's capability explains why the Coast Guard sonar failed to detect them."

"Actually, I don't think the Mexican Coast Guard 's mindset even considered a sub. They were busy searching surface vessels." Serge opined.

"How did the Cubans learn to drive a sub?"

"Russians trained them at their naval base in Santiago. Recall the 'Cuban missile crisis?"

"What's this all about, Biff?"

"Vengeance, Castro's payback. Never proved Cuban involvement in JFK's assassination. He's dying for one more shot at the "imperialists', literally and figuratively. Seethed for decades over our blockade and his country's economic failure under the communist central planning. He never understood capitalism's success. Loathes us, can't understand our success."

"An enormous amount of planning went into this nefarious plot. A successful bioterrorist attack would dwarf 9/11." Serge commented.

"I suspect that sub off loaded the terrorists last night with the Anthrax. Probably came ashore in the Zodiac, hooked up with a prearranged, experienced coyote and are now headed north across the desert. I'm afraid that we just missed them again, Serge!"

CHAPTER THIRTY
GUADALAJARA BOUND – THURSDAY

At three am sharp, the commander brought his sub up to just below the sea's surface. The submarine's periscope picked up the 'all clear' code, flashing from the sandy shoreline five miles north of Puerto Penasco, the designated rendezvous site.

Before the 'all clear' sighting, the sub lay one quarter of a mile offshore in five fathoms of sea in a deep bay devoid of dangerous reefs. Receiving the designated signal, the grizzled Cuban Captain gave the order that Ricardo Sandoval had been waiting for…

"Standby to surface!"

The Cuban crew manned their stations, at the ready.

Moments later the powerful Kilo class submarine broke the surface, like a huge whale breaching, creating huge, splashing waves. A seaman scampered up the conning tower's ladder to open the hatch to check the deck.

"All clear to open the forward hatch," he announced.

Refreshing fresh air rushed into the hatches driven by the steady, ten knot, easterly sea breeze, replacing the stale, damp air in the cramped quarters of the old sub. The poorly functioning a/c system made the all night, underwater trip from the rendezvous island up the Sea of Cortez uncomfortable, obviously a base maintenance oversight in Manzanillo.

"Only a dedicated sailor would tolerate these rugged conditions." It was an uncomfortable trip for the others, but, especially Ricardo Sandoval.

Upon boarding the sub at midnight, Sandoval asked the Captain, "How in the Hell do you breathe down here under water?" He was apprehensive.

The seasoned Captain smiled, "We have a system. Normally we'd snorkel fresh air in, running under the surface. But, for security reasons we choose to run silent and deep to avoid detection. Running on our electronic power is much safer. On sonar radar we would appear as a big whale, if they luckily happened to sight us. Highly unlikely. So, in this case, we get our oxygen by extracting it from sea water by a process of electrolysis. The cabin's CO_2 and toxic fumes are removed by a scrubber."

"A scrubber?" Sandoval enquired.

The Captain patiently explained, thinking, "This weird looking dude sure asks a lot of questions! Better to reassure him, rather than having him freak out." He smiled reassuringly, and explained in relatively non-technical terms.

"It's a simple, chemical engineering process. The scrubber sucks in the stale cabin air, runs it through heated soda lime to absorb the CO_2, then through a charcoal packed bed to remove the CO_2, then through recycled cool soda lime, finally, four steps later, releasing clean fresh air back into the sub's cabin. Got it?"

Sandoval looked puzzled. "I'll take your word for it."

The Captain smiled and returned to his duties.

Everyone looked forward to stretching their legs and breathing fresh morning air, especially Ricardo, who not only was claustrophobic, but coming down with a cold, coughing the entire trip. He could not wait to reach shore, turn the Cubans and their damned canisters over to the waiting coyote, collect his twenty five mil, and head for Guadalajara. If he never saw another Cuban, or sub the rest of his life, he'd be a happy man.

The Zodiac was inflated on the submarine's deck, and after two short trips ashore later, all six men were loading their illicit goods into a large SUV and a jeep with the assistance of the coyote and his two drivers. The two Cubans' eyes never left the three assigned 'special' green stainless steel containers, packed separately in the back of the jeep. The final leg of their sinister mission awaited them, the desert trek led by a "coyote."

Off to the side stood a lanky elderly, physically fit man with a quite distinguished appearance, dressed in a freshly pressed khaki outfit, sporting a classy Caribbean straw fedora with a colorful madras band. He was smoking an expensive Cuban cigar, Cohiba's best. He had reason to celebrate.

He was the overlord of this so far successful caper. The middleman in this covert operation, a co-conspirator in this sinister bioterrorist plot. And... the next in line for Director of Cuba's secret service.

Established in 1961 under the guidance of the Soviet KGB following the Bay of Pigs invasion, the intelligence service represented the Cuban equivalent of the CIA. Comandante Rudolfo Blanco was a 16 year old rifleman defending the Cuban beach that day, almost fifty years ago. Now he was on a different beach engaged in what represented an ongoing lifetime battle with the USA for him and many hardcore Cuban communists.

"Our mission's more than half way there." He murmured to himself.

"Retribution is right around the corner..."

He took great care not to get ashes in his manicured, graying mustache, frequently flicking the ashes away, appearing almost as a nervous habit.

Beside him lay a heavy, tan leather overnight bag with saddle bag side compartments. Behind him a shiny new, light blue Chevy Malibu was parked next to the beach entrance/exit.

Ricardo Sandoval recognized him immediately from their clandestine negotiations over a year ago in Guadalajara. The Comandante was the strategic 'mover and shaker' in this nefarious scheme. It appeared that Rudolfo Blanco would honor their contractual arrangement at Ricardo's first glance.

Ricardo's dream was about to become reality. He spied the new Chevy Malibu and the leather valise by the Cuban operative. He anticipated its contents. He experienced a brief thrill of accomplishment.

As Sandoval approached him, Rudolfo noted the Mexican gangster looked haggard, not well at all. Sandoval was a weird looking hombre to start with. Now he appeared ill.

"Qué tal, Rudolfo?" Ricardo greeted the Cuban operative cordially without an embrazo. This was strictly business.

"Bien, Ricardo." he replied aloofly, almost condescending.

It was obvious that they would not become pen pals. They shared a mutual distaste for each other. But each required the other's services and expertise, a 'marriage of convenience.'

This Mexican cartel jefe represented merely an agent of expediency in his operation. Sandoval had executed his commitment well, time to pay him off, and get the next step of the operation rolling with the coyote that Sandoval so highly recommended. The Comandante never lost sight of his ultimate goal. This major link in the planned chain of events had been successfully completed. Rudolfo had a schedule to meet.

"As agreed, Ricardo, here are the keys to your new Malibu. I'm curious why you chose this car over more upscale models, considering the twenty five million dollars you just made on this deal?"

"This is the car I always rent on my trips to San Diego. Love it. It has sentimental value. I'm not ostentatious. I don't need a fancy car to attract attention. I try to stay under the radar in my line of business."

"I see…" the comandante replied in a noncommittal tone.

"Did he?"… Ricardo wondered.

Comandante Blanco proceeded to conclude their transaction in precise detail. A man of his word.

"The bag contains one million cash in large denomination bills, and certified receipts and activating codes in your name for accounts in three separate banks as requested. Specifically, 15 million in the Cayman Islands, and 4.5 million in each of two banks in Guadalajara. That totals 25 million. Correct?"

"Finally, the bag contains the reservations you requested for a week's vacation at Colima Mountain Resort outside of the city. I believe this finalizes our agreement. Would you care to verify the bag's contents?"

Ricardo hastily examined the bag's contents, verifying that all was in order. He smiled and shook the hand of the Cuban intelligence officer who had kept his part of the deal. He'd soon be heading south in his new Chevy to Guadalajara.

"Gracias, Comandante"

"De nada, Señor."

The Comandante looked him in the eye, questioning his choice of escorts across a treacherous desert with authorities searching everywhere.

"You personally vouch for this coyote's expertise?"...

"Certainly, I do. No reservations. Used him for over twenty years without a mishap. They call him 'Coyote Rex' for good reason. He earned that appellation. He is the absolute best!"

"Rex?..."the Comandante asked with a puzzled look.

"'Rex' is latin for 'king.' Ricardo quickly replied, surprised that this Cuban intel honcho was unfamiliar with this word.

This seemed to reassure the Comandante.

Ricardo gave him back the car keys, surprising him.

"Why are you giving me your keys to the Malibu?"

"I want to say 'good bye' to my men and thank coyote Rex. Please have your driver warm up the Chevy for me."

"An usual request," Rudolfo thought." Strange bird, this Sandoval fellow." He tossed the keys to his driver with the instructions.

Ricardo could hear the Chevy's engine running as he bid his farewells.

"Good. No car bomb set off by the car's ignition. Down the road, I'll check under the hood for C-4 and a detonator timing devise. Ain't taking no chances with these Cuban dudes!"

Ricardo had an innate suspicion of everyone and every circumstance. He trusted no one, especially this Cuban operative who would blow him away in a minute, given the chance.

Now, he could safely head for the next chapter in his life, Guadalajara.

CHAPTER THIRTY ONE

BANKING ON
THE FUTURE – LATE THURSDAY

After a six hour drive, Ricardo Sandoval finally arrived in Guadalajara, frustrated after waiting for three separate car accidents to clear. Traffic backed up for miles. Farm vehicles were involved in all three mishaps in one way or another. Fortunately, no one was killed.

Patience is not a virtue common among Mexican drivers. Horns were blaring, tempers flaring, as drivers leaned out their window swearing at a situation they had absolutely no control over.

"Oughta be a law restricting the hours the damn farmers can use the friggin' highway," he muttered and coughed again. He'd coughed the entire trip, couldn't stop.

"Gotta get some cold medicine in town. Probably caught pneumonia in that damn submarine."

He glanced at his watch," Almost three. Banks and shops would be still be open. Good. No one closed for siesta anymore.

"I've got some important business to attend to this afternoon". He smiled at the thought of opening his bank accounts.

He headed his new Malibu Chevy across the city to the historic central plaza featuring a massive Catholic cathedral, upscale shops, fine restaurants, and a few choice 'hot spots'. He had experienced some of his most enjoyable hours in the plaza. He looked forward to revisiting his favorite tapas bar off the plaza.

Despite his 'cold', his spirits were high, looking forward to a future free from dodging the authorities. Now, with his recently acquired prosperity, he could bank on the future, literally and figuratively.

He glided through the city, familiar with the short cuts, avoiding the tourist spots and popular market places that led to traffic congestion. It was definitely his 'lucky day,' he found a parking place in a couple of minutes, only one half block from the plaza.

"Maybe I should buy a lottery ticket today." It usually took up to an hour of circling around to locate a spot.

Ricardo first stopped at the city's central Banamex. He didn't get in line. Instead, he went directly to the bank manager's office, past his astonished secretary, and, without a word entered the manager's office without knocking. Typical move for him. Ricardo flaunted customary niceties, such as manners.

The bank manager looked up with a surprised expression, thinking, "Who's this weird looking hombre barging into my office, unannounced? 'Señor Cojones'? Ballsy move!"

Ricardo said not a word, pulled up a chair, set down the valise jammed full of cash next to his chair, and sat down in a confrontational fashion…

The manager started to call security. He did not appreciate this dude's attitude, especially with that sneer stuck on his face.

Instead, he said, "How may I be of assistance?"

"I'd like you to expedite a business transaction for me involving a significant sum of money."

He slid the proposed terms of the transaction that he had carefully transcribed from the originals across the desk. The account numbers and coding access identified him as the account 'Trustee'.

"This signifies that you have sole authority to activate an account in our bank, deposited in your name, a sum of 4.5 million dollars, U.S. But, Señor, these are transcribed numbers, do you possess the original certified documents? Some form of identification? Bank regulations require…"

"Cut the bureaucratic bullshit, hombre!" He reached into the leather bag at his side…

"My God! Is he going for a gun?…" the manager flinched in apprehension.

"This should suffice, now get on with it, OK?" he shoved the official papers across to him impatiently.

Relieved this stranger didn't pull a gun on him, he verified the documents. The manager decided to handle this business himself, just to get this demanding S.O.B. out of his bank. This character acted like he had a screw loose. Didn't look well to boot, keeps coughing. Maybe his illness explains his rude, aggressive behavior. Sure hope it's not contagious.

"This will take just a moment, Señor. 'Un momento.'"

He hurriedly typed the essential information into his computer and hit 'send', triggering the electronic transaction. Done.

"My chief teller will deliver a certified copy with all appropriate information for you in about five minutes. Any other service that you require, Señor.?"

"As a matter of fact, I would like to wire transfer one million dollars from the account that you just activated for me to this person's account.'

He gave the wiring instructions to the hassled manager, then suffered another coughing jag.

The concerned manager offered him a box of tissues.

"I hope he doesn't have tuberculosis!" he thought. "Nasty cough."

He examined the wiring instructions.

SEÑORITA ALICIA NICASIO
BANAMEX, CABO SAN LUCAS
ACCOUNT # 8453-311-20

"Saving or checking, Señor?"

"Split it in thirds, between checking, saving, and a jumbo C.D."

"Consider it done, Señor. Since its one of our sister banks, the electronic transaction is complete once I type in these instructions."

He couldn't do enough to hustle this unpleasant hombre out of the bank.

"Anything else I can do for you?" He started to add… "It's been a pleasure…," but refrained.

Most bank managers would have been ecstatic over acquiring an account of this magnitude, but this was a tedious experience he hoped he would not have to endure again. He planned to start locking his door.

"As a matter of fact, there is one more request. It would complicate my life if my ex wife discovered this account. I would appreciate it if you ensure complete confidentiality." Ricardo slipped ten crisp 100 US dollars across the desk to the manager.

Nothing speaks louder in Mexico than a generous 'mordida'.

The bank manager smiled, "That will not be a problem, I assure you Señor Sandoval."

Ricardo Sandoval walked across the plaza to a smaller, rival bank repeating the process a bit more smoothly. The manager there was all over him, delighted to activate such a significant account, no matter how this customer's appearance or attitude came across.

Ricardo had only two more items of business before dinner, wine, and a good cigar. He planned to splurge and then pick up some cold medication.

As Ricardo returned to the other side of the plaza for shopping, a 'spare a peso?' amputee beggar suddenly held out his hand plaintively.

"Por favor, Señor…" interrupting his walk and train of thought. The poor man was a sad sight, destitute, in dirty, ragged clothes. He held out his tin cup to Ricardo, praying for some pocket change.

Ricardo stopped, took off his expensive gold wrist watch and dropped it with a clang into the tin cup.

The amazed beggar thanked him profusely, and 'blessed' him. This spontaneous act of generosity from this sinister appearing stranger brought tears of joy to the beggar's eyes. If he was not disabled, he would have jumped up and hugged this good Samaritan.

"Muchas gracias, Señor."

"Un regalo, amigo. A gift, friend." Ricardo murmured and walked off.

"Vaya con dios!" the beggar shouted after him as he sauntered across the busy plaza.

Ricardo didn't look back. He was getting 'soft'.

He made his way through the crowd to the exclusive jewelry store, quickly selected his item for purchase, plunked down ten thousand cash, and walked out with a brand new Rolex on his wrist.

"Padre Miquel would be proud of me!" he reflected. "I did a good deed today."

CHAPTER THIRTY TWO
SONORAN DESERT JOURNEY – FRIDAY

For late January it was unusually hot and humid. Not the typical dry, 70 degree, pleasant warmth of winter in the Arizona desert. The sun bore down on the six of them, the coyote, two Cubans, and three cartel drug traffickers.

Coyote Rex had picked up his passengers, loaded their contraband, and departed the designated submarine rendezvous beach an hour before dawn. Encountering no traffic traveling north on the two lane highway out of Puerto Penasco, the group made good time.

Ten miles south of the Border Check Point, the SUV and jeep turned sharply onto a winding, rural dirt road, heading NE to an old farm fifteen miles away. It was a bumpy ride, jarring when they hit potholes at forty mph.

This was no ordinary farm, it was the fourth generation homestead of Ubaldo Jimenez who fought in the 1910 Mexican Revolution. The war lasted ten years, but resulted in beneficial social and economic changes. Peasants and the common poor were permitted to acquire land for a pittance.

These fifty arid acres of the Altar Desert were bequeathed to Ubaldo in recognition for his ten loyal years of fighting with Madero and Zapata. Actually, no one else wanted the land. It had meager water, and was located in one of the hottest, most remote, and driest sections of the greater Sonoran Desert.

Coyote Rex, whose Christian name was the same as his great grand-father's, used the farm as a staging post, a jumping off point for the smuggling business into the States. The farm was so remote that no one ever suspected any nefarious activity. For three generations his family barely made a living, but his generation, the fourth, was making a 'killing'. He stood to earn one half million upon successful delivery of the Cubans and the cargo at 'ground zero'. This sum represented ten times his usual fee he commanded as the 'top dog' coyote.

Rex arranged for three pack mules to be staged on the State side of a secret tunnel, recently dug under the border fence especially for this high stakes operation. The mules were well camouflaged, watered, and fed by one of his 'farmhands' who awaiting his small caravan's arrival. The mules were ready for the treacherous desert journey north.

Rex planned this operation with meticulous detail, considering multiple scenarios and fallback plans. Now the execution lay ahead. He prepared to put twenty years of experience on the line. Rex was determined to prove his reputation as the 'best coyote' was well deserved.

"OK, amigos. Load up the horses, pack the saddle bags, we're moving out."

They arrived at the tunnel after a short six mile ride to the border. Rex had them change into light weight camo's, apply sun lotion, and wear a wide brim straw sombrero.

"Ok, now transfer the supplies to the three mules. I have plenty of water, Gatorade, granola and energy bars. Once we strike out, we must continue moving. Be alert to my commands, if you care to survive!"

"Things happen fast in the desert. The rattlesnakes should be hibernating, but be on the lookout. Some may venture out in this unusually hot weather. The sand and decomposed granite are slippery, watch your footing. If you break your ankle and cannot keep up, I'll leave you to your fate with some water. Got it?"

The cartel acknowledged his directives, the trip wasn't their first rodeo. The Cubans just nodded. This was new to them. They trusted that this coyote knew what he was doing. No way they could accomplish the trek without his expert guidance. It would be folly! Their initial impression of the desert amazed them. They had never seen anything like this!

There were no deserts like this in Cuba. The contrast in terrain almost overwhelmed them, coming from a tropical Caribbean island. They never imagined such a vast expanse of crusty brown sand, decomposed granite, and strange vegetation existed. The Sonoran desert did not remotely resemble a 'sand box', or deserts they had seen in movies.

This was harsh landscape, with hills, valleys, ravines, and rocky out cropping. They considered the formidable journey awaiting them in this oppressive heat, the sun rarely disappearing behind a cloud, boring down on them. Wondering what challenges lay ahead, they resigned to plow through it to accomplish their deadly mission, whatever the task required of them.

They set out with a brisk pace that after a few hours, slowed to a saunter, as the unrelenting heat sapped their initial burst of energy. Rex ordered a water break. They had made good progress so far, but he needed to rally them to maintain momentum. It was essential not to bog down, to avoid discovery. "All the slow rabbits were caught", he informed them.

"Not a happy bunch." He noted that unspoken tension existed between the cartel and the Cubans. "What's that all about? Not a good sign."

His caravan rarely spoke. No team spirit prevailed. The Cubans stayed close to the mule carrying their three canisters, seemingly obsessed with their security.

Over the years, Rex had escorted braceros, drug and weapon traffickers, and just plain, poor souls looking for a better life in America. All looking to make a buck. A consistent observation that Rex noticed was that they all showed an upbeat, positive attitude, optimistic about their future. They were willing to accept all risks to gain a better life.

"Certainly not these guys!" Rex observed.

"These hombres are different. Can't put my finger on it. Different focus, different objectives? Who knows? Why should I care? I'm making big bucks, WTF!"

"OK, hombres, let's pick up the pace! Gotta long way to go before night fall."

Surprising that they responded so quickly, Rex commended them.

"That's more like it! For awhile, I thought I was leading a bunch of old ladies to church!"

He laughed at his joke, trying to inject some levity into this dour, incompatible group. The cartel men chuckled, the Cubans never broke a smile.

"Maybe living on an island like Cuba made you lose your sense of humor," Rex reflected.

Rex pushed the group along, part cheerleader, part drill sergeant. Up one hill, down another. Through valleys, gullies, across deep arroyos, followed by steep climbs up embankments. He was a taskmaster, a wiry 150 muscular pounds of infinite energy. He soon had them enervated, sweating profusely, hoping for a refreshing break.

"No need to beat a tired horse," Rex granted them a break. They were not woozies, just out of condition for such strenuous exercise the harsh conditions demanded. He encouraged them to drink some Gatorade to replenish their body salts.

Just as they were about revived, he gave the order.

"OK, Time to move out! Got a flat, sandy stretch coming up about one mile over the next hill. "He pointed in the NE direction.

"Hill? Looks like a frigging mountain to me!" one drug trafficker mumbled.

Up they climbed, the cartel grunting, groaning, and swearing, "Why in the Hell did we take this route?"

Rex noted that, in contrast, the Cubans appeared intransigent, plugging along without comment.

"Tough bastards! Hanging in there."

After 20 arduous minutes, they reached the hill's summit, flattening out onto a wide plateau. It was the first wide open, level desert they had seen.

"OK, take a short break in the shade over there by that stand of palo verde trees. We have a flat section along a deep arroyo for the next five miles. Should be easy going after that last climb. We'll pick up some good time. Keep up the pace, OK?"

The men collapsed in the shade, drinking more water. Rex had warned them of the hazards of dehydration in the desert, a sure 'kiss of death!'

Rex had forgotten how demanding this isolated trail across the desert really was. It had been over a year since he last used it. He chose it because he figured the Border Patrol would least suspect them in this location. The inhospitable terrain was almost a prohibitive challenge in this arid climate, especially for poorly conditioned novices. Frankly, he was pleasantly surprised his caravan had performed so well to this point. So far, so good.

Rex watered his mules, and wondered why camels never caught on for desert travel in the southwest? They would be a good fit.

"Maybe I should look into that idea."

"Time to move out, hombres, up and at 'em!" Rex commanded, just as they were regaining their energy.

A few disgruntled moans later, they resumed their Sonoran journey. It was late afternoon, the hottest time in the desert. They all looked forward towards sundown, a cooler evening. This was much tougher than anyone anticipated. Aptly described by one cartel member, "This is a Bitch, man!"

Several moments later, Rex heard a distant, familiar humming noise in the sky, approaching from the east. The sound struck fear in his heart!

"Drone!" He shouted excitedly.

"Take cover immediately! Get the mules and every one out of sight! The drone will be here in a minute."

All responded immediately to his urgent command. But, unfortunately there is not much cover in the middle of the desert, especially for mules and men.

CHAPTER THIRTY THREE

DRONE COMMAND POST – CLASSIFIED LOCATION IN UTAH FRIDAY AFTERNOON

"There they are! Got em! Check out the screen, 11 o'clock. Just up the trail from the paloverdes trees, lateral to the arroyo to the east. Six of them and three pack mules."

The unmanned drone's high tech cameras' resolution can spot a milk carton from high altitude, relaying the full picture in real time to ground control operators. For 10 million a drone, they were a Pentagon bargain.

Capable of 30 hours in the air without refueling, the drone represented a major surveillance deterrent to the bioterrorist plot in "Operation Roadrunner." If shot down, no pilot or navigator was lost, a low risk, high reward proposition.

Recognizing a National emergency, Homeland Security authorized six drones to pore over the SW desert with hi-tech scrutiny. It appeared this strategy was about to pay big time dividends.

"Roger that. Take 'em out?" the gunner asked.

"That's the standing order. No need to check with D.C. or Langley. Our instructions are to 'find them, and kill them" without concern for collateral damage"

"Take 'em out now. Fire!"

The gunner fired a remote controlled, laser guided, 'Hellfire' missile at the group who were rapidly scattering, diving for cover, obviously hearing the drone's approach.

The huge explosion rocked the desert floor, sending debris and body fragments into the air. A large, dark cloud billowed from the desert floor, obscuring the controller's screen for a few moments.

"When the dust settles, fly by for a close damage assessment," the controller ordered.

A minute later, the drone's cameras relayed the damage in real time.

"Three mangled bodies and the remnants of three mules, plus a lot of debris. But, it looks like three got away! No info on the terrorists' canisters."

"Relay the strike coordinates stat to 'Roadrunner' command. Need a Swat team or commando platoon on the ground to confirm damage. Locate the three who somehow escaped. Request two choppers. Take Anthrax contamination precautions. Get 'search and destroy' platoon in action. They cannot be too far away and are probably wounded."

"Yes, sir. Right away, sir.

"Operation Roadrunner, Come in..."

"Hear you loud and clear."

"Just blew up suspects' caravan. Three bad guys got away somehow..."
"Saw the relay on our monitor. Nice job. Can't believe three men survived that drone missile strike! A direct hit! Doubt they will get far."

"Request ground support, Swat team, platoon strength. Two choppers for close air support. Here are the strike point coordinates."

"Anticipated your request. Mobilizing as we speak."

Ten minutes later, two helicopters took off their pads at Luke AFB, Loaded with a military platoon, armed to their teeth.

On the other side of the base, two F-16's with guided missiles were standing by, awaiting orders, should the platoon locate the three fugitive survivors.

All they needed to blow them to smithereens were the precise coordinates. With their air speed, they could reach the Sonoran desert in minutes.

CHAPTER THIRTY FOUR

CLOSE CALL – FRIDAY PM

Instinctively, hearing the approaching drone, Rex shouted his warning, "Drone!" Then ran for his life, heading for the arroyo 20 feet away. The two Cuban commandos reacted instantly, following Rex, figuring the coyote was their key to survival.

One conscientious Cuban had the brilliant presence of mind to grab one deadly canister, absolutely essential to the mission, off the mule before taking off full speed after the other two men.

Without hesitation, they dived over the arroyos' edge, shoulder rolling down the steep incline's slope covered with rocks, rough gravel, and cacti. They rolled down the hill into the deep arroyo. Their desperate roll hurt like Hell, abrading and bruising them, but not breaking any bones. Before they hit bottom they heard the massive explosion of the drone's missile above the hill, and felt its concussion 100 yards away!

The less fortunate, slow to react cartel members and the mules never knew what hit them, blown away!

"Close call, amigos! Get up and move out! The drone will soon circle to assess damage. We must escape quickly!" Rex ordered.

One Cuban could not get up. He was stuck in a cholla cactus and could not move his injured left arm.

His compatriot went over and pulled him up and off the cactus. He quickly examined his friend's shoulder, determining that it was dislocated.

Without hesitation or discussion, he grabbed his buddy's left arm, put his boot in his armpit, and pulled vigorously.

"Ugg..Dolor! The injured Cuban moaned, as his shoulder joint snapped back in place.

"Vamanos!" Let's go! The rescuing Cuban demanded as he picked up the canister. They took off full speed after Coyote Rex, who was already 100 yards down the arroyo. In a survival mode, they ran a mile as fast as they possibly could, adrenalin pumping, gasping for air. Their life hung in the balance.

"These Cubans are tough dudes," Rex noted. "Underestimated them."

He did not realize that they were hardcore commandos who completed their rigorous training at the top of the class. They did not know the territory, the coyote did. But, they were in top shape. Together the three would strive to elude the drone and the search squads they knew would follow. The hunt was on in earnest.

Rex spotted an outcropping of boulders about 300 yards away. He continued running, pointing out that objective to the Cubans. It looked like a safe place to catch their breath and regroup.

Reaching the boulders, they found a small, cool cave, a stroke of good luck. They could rest briefly, hopefully able to time their escape, incrementally in short dashes, between the drone flyovers.

Rex sensed the hunt would intensify. He knew that the authorities would put troops on the ground to pursue them. They must put as much distance between them and the pursuers as possible. After dark he had confidence that he could elude them. The sun was setting. Darkness would soon be in their favor.

After dark, Rex's expertise would determine the outcome of this contest. No one had matched his skills thus far. But, then again, no one had fired a laser guided missile at him before today! Maybe he was in uncharted territory. He hoped not.

Rex had achieved mythical status as a coyote. His reputation ranked him a 'folk hero' among his peers. This encounter would test his mettle. Determine his legacy. Rex relished the challenge. He knew the desert like his namesake, the coyote. Rex pondered the present predicament that were experiencing.

"What the Hell is in that steel canister that triggered such an overwhelming response? Must be pretty important to bring all this shit down on them!"

"Maybe that is why the Cubans are offering me a half million dollars to deliver these two Cubans to their destination. What in the Hell did Ricardo Sandoval get me into? This sure isn't a routine pot run!"

These thoughts ran through Rex's mind. "All Hell is breaking loose!"

Rex was puzzled that the Cubans did not appear upset that the two other canisters were blown up.

"Guess one will suffice. Bet your sweet ass they won't tell me!"

Suddenly, the Cuban who had his shoulder dislocated jumped up, swatting himself like a madman, swearing.

He inadvertently had reclined on a fire ant colony in the cave, and now the ants were in a full attack mode.

Rex and the other Cuban rushed to his aid.

"Quick, move away! Take off your shirt and pants" Rex demanded.

The Cuban did as told. The ants were biting like mad. Too many bites could kill a man. These ants were venomous.

Rex beat the clothes up against the boulders, shaking the tormenting ants off. He handed the clothes back to the perplexed Cuban with the comment, "You're having a bad day, amigo!" Rex remarked with a smile.

The Cuban didn't whine, he toughed it out.

"Gracias, Rex," he gratefully offered, a rare show of appreciation.

A moment later, Coyote Rex heard the mechanical whine of helicopter blades over a mile away at the missile site. He knew what that meant. Ground troops joining the fray. The hunt's intensity was escalating.

It was almost dusk. They could not hang out here much longer. The troops would track them. Rex consulted his topographical map. He made his decision and explained it in great detail to the Cubans who now trusted his judgment implicitly.

"OK, listen up. Here's my plan…"

CHAPTER THIRTY FIVE

THE MISSILE SITE — SONORAN DESERT — FRIDAY AT DUSK

"**C**ome in 'Operation Roadrunner', this is team Pima Bravo…"

"Hear you loud and clear, Bravo. Go on …"

"Landed both choppers at the missile strike site. Big time crater, a lot of destruction. Direct hit took out three men, three mules, supplies and contraband."

"Any sign of the canisters?'

"We found some stainless steel green fragments, impossible to reconstruct."

"So, we don't know if all three Anthrax canisters were destroyed, do we?"

"That is affirmative,…correct, sir."

"We must assume that the three escapees took one or two canisters with them…"

"That's a command decision, sir…"

"Sorry, Lt. I was thinking out loud."

"Understand, sir."

"Any sign of those who got away?"

"Platoon deployed, as we speak, sir."

"Almost night fall, get on it!"

"Roger that, sir."

"Lt, are all the men taking Anthrax contamination precautions?"

"Yes, sir. Gloves, masks, all men started on Cipro…"

"Good man, Lt. Keep us posted. Frequent updates. OK?"

"Yes, sir."

"We plan to augment your ground search and pursuit into the night with drone and helicopter aerial surveillance. We'll see how effective our new special night vision gear is. Maybe it will live up to the hype. Stay on it Lt. I don't have to emphasize how much is at stake."

"Where do you think they are heading, sir. Phoenix or Tucson? Maybe we could set up an ambush."

"Phoenix. Think they are going to a ballgame…over and out."

"A ballgame?" This statement really puzzled the Lt.!

CHAPTER THIRTY SIX

SLIPPING AWAY INTO
THE NIGHT – FRIDAY NIGHT

"**O**K, we are in deep trouble. Choppers just landed where the drone missile blew up our caravan. They will soon figure out that we are missing, escaped the explosion. They'll be hot in our trail. I mean 'shoot to kill hot.' No questions asked. It's almost dark. We have a small window of opportunity, but cannot afford any screw ups. Got it?"

"OK, let's go!"

They quickly climbed the far ridge, up and out of the arroyo in an easterly direction. They hid out of sight in another pile of huge boulders, anticipating a drone flyby. Five minutes later a drone flew directly overhead. They patiently waited. Now, time for another sprint.

"The drone will keep circling. When it disappears over the north ridge, run as fast as you can to those Paloverde trees, about 1000 yards away." He pointed out the direction to the Cubans.

"Plan to strike out running in about five minutes. OK? I'll give you the go sign. Be ready."

Coyote Rex never faced a challenge like this. The drone attack changed his game plan. He must abandon his proposed route, and backtrack ten miles through some of the most inhospitable, rugged desert terrain on earth.

It would be a brutal, all night trek. But, it was their only hope. The authorities would never suspect anyone would be crazy enough to attempt such a stunt, especially at night.

"Only a few plastic bottles of water left in our backpacks. We must reach our destination tonight, before daylight. Otherwise, we'll die of dehydration, or be captured or killed!" Rex instructed them.

Even for a coyote of his vast experience, this represented a supreme challenge.

Rex had developed a new respect for the Cubans.

"Tough, gritty, not whiners…Those traits will come in handy tonight", he thought to himself.

"Ready, hombres? Run like the devil is after you!"

Exhausted from the long sprint to the trees, they collapsed, breathing heavily, on the ground under the foliage's cover.

"How long will this go on? Worse than boot camp!" The Cubans thought.

"Made it, Hombres!" Rex proudly announced the obvious, smiling.

The Cubans responded only with a thin smile, to beat to talk. This coyote was wearing them out. They envied his stamina.

"How's he do it?" they wondered.

Coyote Rex had one more trick in his bag. He was not 'a one trick pony.'

On the routine drug runs he never carried a cell phone, fearing the authorities would track his GPS signal. On this special mission, however, he made an exception to his rule. Since he planned to use a route seldom traveled, thus less patrolled, he brought his cell phone to facilitate meeting up with Luis, the intermediary in this operation, whom he didn't know, at a rendezvous point, that he was also unfamiliar with, somewhere near Tollison, a west Phoenix suburb. Probably, not a smart idea in retrospect, but the cell phone might now serve a useful purpose.

The drone attack radically altered his plans. He didn't expect escorting two Cubans with their canisters across the Sonoran desert would bring down the wrath of the USAF, Border Patrol, ATF, and the DEA!

"Holy shit! WTF!" Rex rarely swore, but this was a unique event in his life, unreal!

He felt like he was in some kind of weird action film. Detached. This could not really be happening. He could accept them trying to capture them. That was a 'cops and robbers' thing that he and other coyotes were accustomed to, but drone missiles? A bit of an overkill, maybe?"

"Give me a break!" he mumbled to himself. "What's this all about?"

"Whatever we're transporting, the Americans want real bad." Rex reflected. "Willing to kill us for that container!"

"Wonder how much that friggin' missile cost 'em? Those guys are really bringing it on!"

Rex decided to use the cell phone as a decoy. He scrubbed the phone's information, hiked two hundred yards down to another ravine, placing the phone on top of a boulder. Its GPS signal should soon attract attention, buying some time for them to take off in another direction.

"A flyby will pick up its signal and divert efforts in this direction while we take off in the opposite way. Should buy us some time," he informed the Cubans, who were still breathing heavily.

"OK, listen up. There is old, deserted feed barn two miles or so east of here. It's dark now, follow me. Be alert for drones and helicopters. Doubt anyone will tract us on foot where we are headed. So far, we are beating the odds. That's what this is all about, hombres." He addressed them like a foot General, trying to inspire them.

What other choices did they have? You bet they'd follow him!

Under the cloak of night they made their way to the barn, rested, sparingly drank some water, then resumed their journey across some incredibly formidable desert terrain that nobody in their right mind would attempt. Precisely why Coyote Rex chose this route.

For the next five hours they slipped away into the night, undetected.

CHAPTER THIRTY SEVEN
"RED ROOSTER" – FRIDAY MIDNIGHT

"'Red rooster', 'Red rooster', come in..."

"Read you loud and clear, 'Roadrunner'..."

"How's the recon going? ..."

Six helicopters were flying rotating grid recon patterns across the SW desert. Equipped with modern night vision and infrared gear they combed the wide area around the drone missile strike, assuming the three survivors were wounded, or unable to escape the immediate surrounding area because of the formidable terrain. They were convinced that they would soon capture or kill the fugitive terrorists. It was just a matter of time. They were closing the noose around their necks. The chase would soon be over. Absolutely no way they could escape.

The command chopper responded," No luck yet. A lot of wild life, no bad guys. Moon coming up, we'll get a little more illumination."

"They couldn't just vanish into thin air. Keep up your pursuit and keep us in the loop."

"Roger that, over and out."

Ten minutes later. "Roadrunner, come in..."

"Read you. Rooster..."

"Picked up a GPS signal, three and one half miles NE of strike site. Jot down these coordinates... Request permission to go in with back up."

"You got it, Rooster. Be careful, we are sure they are armed, and we know they're dangerous."

"No match for our M-16's. Goin' in…"

The attack helicopter touched down on the only relatively flat spot within 100 yards of the GPS signal. Four heavily armed commandos in kevlar vests and helmets scurried down the steep, treacherous bank, M-16's ready to engage the bad guys. The chopper's flood lights Illuminated their path. They quickly evaluated the situation and radioed in their findings.

"No sign of them. Check those coordinates again, Captain."

"Still getting a strong signal. You must be right on top of it. Check out those boulders over to your right."

"Look over here, Sgt. On top of the rock. Odd place to leave your cell phone."

"Careful! Could be booby trapped. Look for C-4, a detonator, trip wires … be careful!"

After a moment, "All clear." He tossed the phone to the Sgt. who checked it out.

"Phone's been scrubbed. Notify 'Roadrunner. Clever. They set up a decoy"

"Roadrunner, come in…"

"Read you, Rooster…What's up?"

"They left a cell phone as a decoy! Scrubbed the phone."

"Bring it in. Our tech's will reconstruct it. Suspect it contains some valuable information and leads. Obviously, we are dealing with a wiley coyote who set us up with a cunning diversion. Bought 'em some time, so instruct your squadron to increase the perimeter grid pattern. Doubt they headed due east. That would be suicidal at night, crazy. Rugged slog. So, concentrate on the NE routes these characters usually take."

"Roger. Keep you posted, Roadrunner."

Rex could hear the helicopters intensely searching for them 10 to 15 miles to the NE of their position. Sound carries across the desert with no interference, except for the occasional howl of coyotes.

This reinforced his determination. He had made the wise decision. They plugged onward, across grueling desert wilderness.

The Cubans kept up, not saying a word, concentrating on the daunting task. Rex occasionally rallied them on with encouraging remarks.

"Red Rooster, Come in…What's happening?"

"Nothing, Roadrunner. No sign of them! Covered the area like a blanket, Commander."

"Think they deviated eastward into no man's land? That's like the moon with cacti!"

"At night? That would be sheer folly! But, I realize that we are dealing with a shrewd Coyote. Probably a good idea to send a couple of choppers over there to scout it out. Whata ya think, Commander?"

"Do it, Captain. Happy hunting!"

"You got it, Commander. We're on it."

Meanwhile, Rex pressed on, encouraging the Cubans that they were only two hours from the rendezvous with Luis, according to his calculations.

"Hang in there, amigos. We are going to make it!"

He now referred to them in a friendly fashion, rather than simply calling them non-flattering "hombres." The Cubans' perseverance earned his respect, if not admiration.

Suddenly, Rex heard the harsh, whirling blades of approaching helicopters, coming in fast. The choppers would be on them in less than 3 or 4 minutes at their airspeed.

"Take cover, get low over there under those rocks. Lie on top of your canister. Their instruments will pick up the metal."

Hardly a necessary command. The Cuban had cradled it like a baby since the drone attack, up and down hills, across ravines, even climbing rock piles up and out of a steep canyon.

"See anything? Shine your spotlights down the arroyos. Spot any infrared images?"

"Just some coyotes, the four legged kind." The crew snickered.

When the choppers flew right over them at 500 feet and did not circle back, Rex knew they were home free. The rocks saved them.

"Come in, Red Rooster …"

"Read you, 'Runner…"

"Any luck?"

"No sir. They either disappeared off the face of the earth, slipped away in the night, or died under a rock."

"Like poltergeist! Keep searching. They're out there somewhere.

The drones are refueling at Luke. They will be back in the fray in an hour."

Rex pressed on, Cubans in tow. Ducking for cover whenever they heard a chopper, but one never got close again.

Rex consulted the notes on his map regarding the designated meeting place with Luis, set at 5 am.

"Good. Only one quarter of a mile to go." He glanced at his wrist watch, 4.30 am. Plenty of time.

He took out his night vision binoc goggles. There it was, an old blue Chevy Belaire.

A tall, skinny Latino leaned against the car, smoking a cigarette. He did not know what Luis looked like, but Rex knew the blue Chevy was the signal.

"Home free!" Rex exulted.

They had made it against formidable odds!

Rex 's net worth would soon go up dramatically to the tune of one half million dollars, deposited electronically in a Guadalajara Banamex in his name, as soon as he delivered the Cubans and their cargo safely.

Luis' instructions were to activate Rex's account by sending the encrypted code on his Blackberry. This information automatically would be relayed to the Santiago Naval Base in Cuba.

He informed the Cubans of the good news.

"You will shower and sleep in a soft bed tonight after a few ice cold beers, of course. Our rendezvous with Luis is 15 minutes away.

The Cubans not only smiled, but shook his hand and offered their sincere gratitude with a genuine, warm embrazo.

"Gracias, Coyote Rex!"

CHAPTER THIRTY EIGHT

FBI REGIONAL HEADQUARTERS, PHOENIX — SATURDAY 10 AM

The regional director of the FBI, Eduardo Trujillo-Evans, presided over a hushed, concerned group of National Security advisors in the twenty first floor penthouse conference room. Not unexpected, group rivalries engendered some contentious discussion. There was the usual amount of bickering, jockeying for position, and, most importantly, avoiding blame.

The Cuban terrorists and a coyote guide had incredibly slipped through a desert snare of six drones, six attack helicopters, and a small platoon of commandos. The questions posed to the director were, "How in the Hell could this possibly happen?"

"Did the drone's laser guided missile destroy the three deadly Anthrax canisters?"

"Did the Bioterrorist threat still exist?"

The director maintained his poise. He was the committee's host, coordinating 'Operation Roadrunner' among the different agencies, namely, Homeland Security, CIA, DEA, ATF, Border Patrol, and the county sheriff and police departments. All had their agendas, turfs, and special interests.

Eduardo felt like he had been assigned to 'herd rabbits'. A lot of ego's involved in this operation. He may step on a few toes getting the job done, but he was putting forth a tremendous effort to coordinate interagency assignments and responsibilities to thwart an impending bioterrorist attack. They all respected his leadership.

"Let me address the three vital questions in order, briefly, based on our current information and intelligence reports."

"Number one, how did they pull off this remarkable escape through a rugged desert against such overwhelming odds, manpower, and technology?"

"Simply never underestimate the power of human ingenuity and willpower to succeed. My staff's research suggests that this particular coyote possesses almost superhuman survival instincts and stamina, much like the wild animal he is named after. The coyote manages quite well in the wilderness, in fact thrives, if I may use that analogy. All indications point to 'Coyote Rex' in this case, an exceptionally skilled and experienced guide."

The conference crowd shifted in their seats, wondering, 'Coyote Rex? What's that all about? Sounds like something out of a Hollywood script... an 'extraordinary coyote', a desert guide?"...

All were puzzled, except the Border Patrol. They certainly knew who this particular coyote was that the director was talking about. Rex had eluded capture numerous times over the last 20 years, always just when they thought had him cornered and about to be nabbed. Rex managed to stay one step ahead of them. This coyote was one clever devil! They suspected Rex was involved in this 'getaway' from the start. It bore all of his phenomenal hallmarks. Rex's legendary maneuvers in the SW desert had become folklore. The Border Patrol had a certain respect for him in a 'counter-culture' way.

The FBI director concluded his answer to question number one with the remark, "I think on the basis of his recent desert performance the coyote has earned the appellation, 'Rex', latin for 'King.' "

"Now to address the second question on the floor, regarding the hypothetical, 'Did the missile blast destroy all the deadly Anthrax?'"

"Evidence at the explosion site documented green, stainless steel fragments contaminated with Anthrax spores microscopically. So we know with certainty that at least one canister was blown up. But, it would be an unfair, illogical, and dangerous supposition to assume all three canisters were destroyed. That would imply that the Bioterrorist threat no longer exists."

"That essentially answers question number three, 'Does a credible Bioterrorist threat still exist?'"

"Absolutely! Now we are confronted with developing a strategy to avert a National disaster that potentially exceeds 9/11 in physical and psychological impact."

Dr. Emil Chamberlain, the renowned Bioterrorism expert from the Fort Diechtrich Lab in Maryland, nodded his head in agreement.

"We are facing a 'Doomsday' scenario. We need to make some critical decisions this morning. The floor is open for discussion."

A spirited exchange of ideas ensued between these experienced security officials.

Biff Roberts and fellow CIA officer, Serge Betancourt listened carefully in the back of the conference room. They 'had a dog in this fight.' They had chased the 'bad guys' all the way from Cabo San Lucas.

Numerous ideas, scenarios, game plans, fallback schemes, plans B were bantered, back and forth. Slow, but constructive progress was being made. It was a tedious process at best.

Biff was not sure everyone would end up on the same page. They were focused on the big picture, the general concepts of interventional tactics.

"What about the 'nitty gritty' of the actual 'takedown', the 'set up'?"

Biff could not restrain himself any longer. In his typical 'this is how we should look at it, and get the job done' manner", he offered his advice.

"I look at this as a 'Willey Sutton' moment."

That 'starter line' got the audience's attention. They all were familiar with Biff's esteemed reputation with the CIA.

"When asked why he robbed all those banks, Willey simply replied, 'That's where all the money is!'"

Consider this analogy, and pretend you were a terrorist. Where would you attack us to achieve maximum damage physically and psychologically?"

"Apply his logic. You would target a large gathering, some place where a crowd is congregated, a community event. Right?" "OK. What's going on this weekend in Phoenix?" I checked the Arizona Republic. Here's the rundown.

NASCAR tomorrow, Sunday afternoon at P.I.R.

NFL playoff tomorrow, Cardinals vs, Cowboys at Glendale stadium.

U2 concert tomorrow evening at U.S. Airways center That is the line up of targets I'd seriously consider hitting, if I was a terrorist."

The Cubans have very cleverly conceived and executed this plot thus far, the sub, the cartel's escort, and coyote's role. Now they need to capitalize on these successes. Go for the 'big kill!' Weapons grade Anthrax requires a system to aerosol the lethal spores into the atmosphere for maximum effectiveness."

"Now, how would you do that, if you were a terrorist?"

The group of security specialists were closely following Biff's line of reasoning, impressed that he may well be the 'smartest man in the room.' Biff continued…

"Take a page out of history, which we all know, has a tendency to repeat itself. Commenting on Pearl Harbor, Harvard Professor Thomas Shelling noted, 'There is a tendency in our planning to confuse the unfamiliar with the improbable.'"

"We must focus on the unknowns, predict the unpredictable by thinking outside the box. Agencies tend to become too insular in our thought processes, too predictable. Not all hoof beats outside the door are horses. Gentlemen, Zebras exist!"

"For the terrorist, life is a one act play. Here is what I think they will do, and actions I propose to prevent their act of terrorism…"

CHAPTER THIRTY NINE
SAFEHOUSE, PHOENIX SUBURB — SATURDAY PM

"**S**o, what'd you think, amigos?"

Luis El Faro had just conducted a mock demonstration of a devise he designed for a sustained, timed release of virulent Anthrax spores.

"We can trigger this devise with a simple cell phone call, avoiding exposing ourselves. Clever, huh?"

The two Cubans seemed impressed with Luis' engineering skills.

"Muy bueno!" Very good!"

They had slept all day, exhausted from the grueling, relentless desert trek, dodging authorities whose sole intention was to kill them. They acknowledged that Coyote Rex had saved their ass, and their mission. They told him so, with an exchange of genuine embrazos, remarkable for these hardcore commandos.

The implacable coyote took off shortly after Luis electronically activated Rex's account in Guadalajara and presented him with the appropriate paperwork. Actually, he did not look too worn out. The little guy was a physical 'giant' with a tenacious drive. No telling where he is now. He turned down Luis' invitation to hang out awhile.

Luis had steaks marinating, promising a BBQ feast after his technical demonstration. The three conspirators were drinking ice cold Coronas, no lime. "Kicking back", as Luis described this pleasant respite.

The Cubans envied Luis' modest, two bed room track home in a blue collar community, with a lawn and a back yard accommodations.

"Some safe house! Luis lives pretty good! Not like home, agree? One Cuban commented to the other.

"Living like a Cuban politician back home," the other replied.

Luis continued to explain his lethal plans, between swigs of beer. He noted the Cubans were fascinated with his contraction.

"After I activate this devise, weapons grade Anthrax spores will aerosol through the stadium's entire ventilation system, filling the atmosphere with a high concentration of lethal Bacilli. The aerosol is invisible and odorless. Once inhaled by the unsuspecting crowd, it will rapidly multiply in their lungs, spreading into the blood stream. Everyone will die before the game is over. And, most first responders will also die, suffering the same fate, without a clue of the cause of death."

"This will freak out and panic the Americans, just like 9/11. No one will know it is Castro's payback. The CIA will trace the genetic marker of the weapons grade Anthrax to the lab in Iran that manufactured and processed the deadly concoction. Then mad as Hell, the U.S. will start another war in the Middle East, this time with Iran. Clever scheme, agree amigos?"

"Fidel will have the last laugh!"

The two Cuban shook their heads in amazement. They knew they were part of a terrorist plot, but certainly not the full extent of Castro's devious scheme. Luis seemed wired in to the plot's overall objectives. They understood the master plan, knew their role, but were not privy to such detailed information.

"How do you know all of this, Luis?"

"Friends of mine in the U.N. in NYC told me, the 'WASPS.'"

"WASPS?" This confused the terrorist hit men.

Luis explained that Cuban spies had operated out of the Cuban mission to the U.N. for years. U.S. intelligence agencies tracked their moves, referring to the Cuban spies by the code name, "WASPS".

Unfortunately, the CIA surveillance team missed the Luis El Faro transaction, setting up this clever bioterrorist scheme about to occur.

This covert 'WASPS' network had recruited Luis six months earlier for this 'special job'. The planning was meticulous. And, the price was right, 250 K cash, 50 K up front. Luis was on board with their wicked intrigue. He had no allegiance to the U.S. In fact, Luis carried a grudge. He could be had, especially for a 'quarter mil'.

Luis was an illegal Arizona immigrant, working under bogus documentation with a fake I.D. and driver's license. His family had been rounded up and deported to Mexico last year. He assumed an alias, grew a beard, and slipped through the E- Verify screening system with falsified documents. Getting a good job was easy after that.

Luis like many 'illegal's' resorted to 'sources' in Phoenix specializing in documentation. Gaming the system was an art science to these specialists. For 5 K they performed a pro job for Luis and his two "Cuban cousins" expected to arrive later on in the year, 'probably in January', Luis informed them. They could take passport photos then to attach to their bogus documents.

With his mechanical skills, Luis had no trouble landing a job with 'Glendale A/C and Plumbing, LLC.' This company was the licensed contractor for Glendale's new state of the art football stadium.

Not a strange coincidence.

Luis El Faro had authorized access to the stadium's central A/C and ventilation system. In fact, Luis routinely checked out the system every Sunday morning before the game.

CHAPTER FORTY
COLIMA MOUNTAIN RESORT, GUADALAJARA — SATURDAY PM

"It's got to be the altitude! I never wheeze." Ricardo Sandoval exclaimed. "Otherwise, I wouldn't be this short of breath. I'm huffing and puffing between coughs."

"Four thousand meters is really not that high. Probably just aggravating my bad cold. That medicine I bought doesn't seem to be working."

He had been listless all day, following a restless Friday night in the resort's luxurious Presidential suite. He tossed and turned with occasional fever and chills. The resort's food and service were top notch, but he was too enervated, not up to eating or drinking much. Ricardo felt 'just plain whipped!'

His lunch remained untouched on the suites' dining room table, accompanied by the expensive wine that he had ordered decanted.

"Probably caught pneumonia in that damn cold and damp submarine. Definitely, an unpleasant experience in those cramped quarters. I think that I'd go nuts in that job!" He murmured to himself.

He started coughing again and could not stop. These spells were annoying the Hell out of him. He had planned to celebrate his fortune and 'retirement' at this exclusive retreat in the mountains, really 'whoop it up'. Now he had to deal with this miserable illness.

"Maybe this is just altitude sickness. I've spent my entire life close to sea level. But, guess I better call the front desk to request they send an errand boy to the pharmacy to buy some antibiotics over the counter, just in case it's a bronchial infection. Better cover all bases. I don't want to spend my vacation like this."

He placed the call, then slumped on the sofa, exhausted from such a minor exertion.

"What's wrong with me?" He wondered and fell asleep.

An hour later the suite's doorbell rang, awakening Ricardo. He looked at his new Rolex wrist watch, five pm. He staggered to the door. It was the resort's errand boy.

"The local pharmacy was closed, Señor Sandoval, due to a death in the family. I wanted to inform you that I must drive to town. It will take a couple of hours at this time of day due to the heavy traffic. Very sorry for the inconvenience, Señor."

"No problem." He gave the young man twenty dollars for his trouble.

Actually, it was indeed a serious problem. His physical condition was deteriorating by the hour. Emotionally, Ricardo experienced difficulty coping with his present situation. Confused as to what was ailing him, Ricardo was becoming miserable and depressed.

"This should be the happiest day of my life, and here I am, 'sick as a dog!'"

He tried to resume his nap, planning a late dinner when he was rested enough to enjoy the meal. The excellent wine he'd ordered for lunch should hold its body. He'd enjoy it with dinner.

An hour later, another coughing spell awoke him. He tried to sit up, but almost fell off the sofa. Uncontrolled, foul smelling, blood tinged sputum rocketed across the tile floor as he coughed forcefully, struggling to clear his airway. Ricardo felt like he was suffocating. He became apprehensive, fearing he needed more air. It frightened him.

He was on fire with a high fever, sweating profusely. A series of shaking chills racked his effete frame.

"Maybe I should go to the hospital and see a Doctor." He thought.

He staggered to the bedroom, opening all the windows to let more air into the suite. Ricardo hungered for air. He hung his head out the window, gulping air into his lungs.

A gentle mountain breeze rustled the light cotton curtains. The winter sun, about to set above the western mountain ridge, cast a long shadow across the verdant, manicured golf course below, a reminder that darkness would soon follow, for the course, and for Ricardo.

Oblivious of the spectacular view, Ricardo steadied his elbows on the tenth story ledge, stuck his head out into the fresh evening air, attempting to suck all the precious oxygen in the atmosphere into his lungs, willing them to breathe for him.

Below, guests were laughing and conversing, enjoying cocktails on the verandas. Tuxedoed waiters scurried. Just yards away, the last foursome of the day approached the 18th green to putt out.

No one noticed Ricardo Sandoval's dire distress ten stories above them in the Presidential suite. Oblivious, they were too busy living, while he was busy dying.

Ricardo managed to make it back across the bedroom from the window sill. He was getting dizzy, afraid he would fall out the window. He stumbled and fell backwards onto the bed.

He wheezed like an asthmatic. He sensed he was losing it, becoming incoherent. Anxiety crept into emotions. Indecision gripped him. Inaction doomed him.

Ricardo was delirious with fever and hypoxia. The room was spinning around him, his life passing before him. He lay on the bed, observing his life events as a spectator, his thoughts fragmented, wandering aimlessly from past to present. Some recollections occurred in slow motion, others in rapid fire frames, all spontaneously, all uncontrolled.

"Landed the deal of a lifetime and can't enjoy it!...Not one lousy minute! ...I'm all alone in this room...Alicia...the only one I ever loved... Where are you?...How are the boys, Jorge?...Why am I so sick?...Where am I?... How did I get in this submarine?...What happened to our Zodiac?... Great Chevy!...What's this floating before my eyes?...Am I losing it?"

Another violent round of uncontrollable coughing hit him. His ribs hurt. This time fresh blood accompanied the foul sputum, soiling the expensive bedcovers. He was burning up, shaking like a leaf. Delusional.

Now panic overcame him. He could hardly breathe, His respirations tugged, trying to capture oxygen, gasping like a fish out of water. Twitching, almost convulsing, desperation overcame him.

He tried to get up, reach the phone, dial 911…Ricardo did not make it. He collapsed on the floor, two feet short of the bedside desk.

Ricardo labored for air. He took one last gasp and sighed, "Alicia…"

His death knell. His denouement.

Moments later, the suite's doorbell rang.

No one answered.

CHAPTER FORTY ONE

UNIVERSITY OF PHOENIX STADIUM, GLENDALE, AZ – SUNDAY AM

"**G**ood morning, Henry."

Luis greeted the stadium's maintenance gate guard, familiarly, as on most Sunday's during the football season. This was the 'big game', the NFL playoffs, Cardinals vs. the Cowboys. Luis arrived a little early, flashing his pass, a ritual for all home games. He was waved through the street side entrance gates, and headed for the special parking for concessions and maintenance.

Luis' job was to insure the stadium's A/C system functioned properly with the retractable roof closed. Even though it was a beautiful late January day, the roof would predictably be shut for two reasons.

To increase the crowd noise, favoring the home team. And, to satisfy the Card's all-star QB 's superstition, that they won more often when the roof was closed.

He pulled the company van up to the lots' restricted gate, flashing his pass nonchalantly to the gate guard, Henry.

"See you got some helpers today, Luis."

Henry peered through the window of the maintenance van, creating some anxiety for the Cubans who instinctively reached for their 45's under their janitorial uniforms.

Luis discreetly gave them a low hand signal, out of Henry's sight, to 'cool it.' It was tense moment.

Henry did not recognize the two Hispanics in coveralls with the company logo on their sleeves. Luis usually came alone.

"Yeah, Henry. Breaking in a couple of new apprentices. Maybe I'll get a weekend off now and then. How cool would that be?"

He laughed casually. He didn't want Henry snooping. All he needed was a shoot out at the gate to blow the mission. A year's planning down the drain. He prayed the Cubans wouldn't get trigger happy. Not here, not now.

The Cubans got his signal, deciding to let Luis handle the unanticipated problem. This was his turf.

"OJT, you know. They need some 'hands on' experience. Can't rely on just workshops to train 'em, you know, Henry."

"Just a formality, Luis, but we are on a high security alert. I know you, but I've got to see your buddies' ID's, OK?"

"No problem, Henry. Got 'em, E- verified, in fact. Papers in glove compartment, hang on just a moment, OK?"

Luis retrieved the documents and handed them to Henry, who examined them carefully, glancing in the van to match the photos with the occupants.

"Their doc's are in order, Luis." He motioned Luis through the check point.

The Cubans sat stone silent and rigid, avoiding eye contact.

"Your buddies don't say much, Luis."

"Their English is a little shaky. Embarrassed, I guess around strangers." He quickly changed subjects.

"Big game today. Can't believe they won't open the retractable roof. Great weather, huh, Henry?"

Luis chatted in a cordial fashion, trying not to appear in a rush. This was' just another Sunday'. The act he portrayed was designed to distract the possibly suspicious guard.

The comment successfully distracted Henry, a rabid football fan.

"You know our QB, Luis. Whatever it takes for him to connect on a long bomb to Fitz." Henry replied, all suspicions gone, with a laugh, waving them through the security gate.

Luis waved and drove slowly away, joining in the laugh.

"Have a good day, Henry."

Both Cubans wondered what was so funny. They were prepared to blow Henry away. They were focused on their deathly mission. Nothing could stop them now.

Luis laughed because the closed roof ironically suited their purpose perfectly, a closed environment would make the lethal aerosol more effective.

Luis maneuvered through the early 'tailgaters', jockeying for choice spots to party in the vast parking lot. He avoided running over loose footballs from multiple, scattered touch football games in the lot.

He headed directly for the maintenance entry, restricted to those with security clearance and authorized keys.

Luis had keys for this door and two others, the private elevator, and the huge A/C control room for the stadium's ventilation system.

He parked the company van close to the door for the planned 'getaway'. He looked around, checking for security guards.

"All clear!" He signaled the Cubans, and grabbed his tool bag. The Cubans jumped out of the van with two large duffle bags bearing the firm's logo. They hustled to the door and slipped safely inside, sight unseen, so they thought. Only two doors to go.

Across the lot, the CIA observed the three men through binoculars, taking telephotos with a high powered Nikon lens camera, documenting the operation's inception.

"That's gotta be them!"

As the three suspects entered the stadium, the CIA's plan swung into action.

The agents signaled the fire truck to move in. The firemen did, quickly barricading the maintenance door with heavy concrete blocks, marking the door officially 'OUT OF ORDER'. No one could enter or, more importantly, no one could exit through this door.

Next, they contacted their team leader who organized this last ditch effort to thwart the terrorists. He had calculated the probabilities correctly. The terrorists' target was indeed the 'ballgame'!

No wonder this man enjoyed such a phenomenal reputation!

"Good call, Biff. Three Latinos dressed in white coveralls, lugging three bags, just entered the maintenance door. Should arrive shortly on the private elevator. Heads up!"

Biff heard the message through his ear piece. He was already inside the stadium, briefing the troops.

"Show time!" he said to Serge standing next to him, with a grin wider than usual.

"Alert the 'janitors', I'll see you later." Biff said as he headed down the hallway out of sight to a predetermined location.

Biff had correctly played the odds that the terrorists would target the ballgame for their 'big kill.' The stadium's ventilation system with the roof shut was such a logical, compelling target.

Biff had put himself in the mass assassin mindset. Given the opportunity, how could any warped mind pass up this chance to inflict maximum physical and psychological impact? A sellout NFL playoff game televised nationally? How more effective to strike terror into the hearts of a nation?

His calculated guess proved an act of providence.

Biff meticulously planned the 'sting' operation. He checked the central ventilation system, the maintenance contract, and the service personnel. The strike team had memorized the stadium's layout.

Biff strategically dispersed armed Swat and Commando teams in critical intercept locations. All were convincingly disguised as janitors or concessionaires. All were briefed on what to anticipate, who and what to look for. And, they had a strict "fire' protocol.

"Stay cool," he advised. "The A/C crew, our targets, just arrived on time, ten am."

All the men were sharpshooters, most combat veterans. They grasped the significance of this "takedown.'" One premature move could compromise the operation, and result in unnecessary casualties.

Serge and four other CIA 'janitors', busily swept the hallway between the service elevator and the central A/C control room, about fifty yards down the tiled hallway.

"They just hopped on the elevator, three Hispanics in overalls. On their way up. Look a little gnarly."

The relayed message rung too loudly in Serge' earpiece.

"WTF!" He dialed down the volume.

He signaled his four operatives. They pretended to resume their sweeping and mopping chores in a convincing manner, next to their service carts.

Serge felt his pulse quicken with excitement, not fear.

"Finally, we've got them!"

The service elevator door opened. The villains stepped out, toting the three bags, thirty yards away. They looked around, checking for security, seeing only janitors. Assured the coast was clear, they proceeded around the corner, up the tiled hallway to the A/C control room unimpeded.

"Easier than we thought", Luis murmured in Spanish to the Cubans.

"Que bueno! How good!" they replied. They were prepared for a confrontation. Things were going very smoothly.

Serge was inclined to kill them right now. It would be a 'piece of cake'.

But, Biff had issued strict orders and clearly stated parameters for this operation. Serge never looked up, nor did his four agents, continuing to clean the hallway before the gates opened soon for the ticket holders to come in.

The three terrorists ignored them at first, heading directly pass them to reach the ventilation control room door down the hall, about fifty yards away.

Half way there, Luis suddenly stopped and looked back, sensing something wasn't quite right with this picture.

"Usually only one janitor on duty at this hour on Sunday morning, not five!" Luis did not recognize them.

"Henry had mentioned a 'security alert'. Had they fallen into a trap?"

He quietly issued orders in Spanish to the Cubans. They were only ten yards from the heavy steel door to the A/C vent room.

Almost instantly, all Hell broke loose!

The Cubans pulled uzzi's from their duffle bags and sprayed the hallway with a hail of bullets in Serge' direction. Luis fired an automatic pistol, emptying the clip, quickly changing to a fully loaded one.

The barrage of bullets ricocheted everywhere in the Hellfire. Off the floor, off the walls, and ceilings.

Two agents fell, wounded before they could retaliate.

Serge ducked behind the service cart, returning fire with his Glock .9 mm. Two of his men immediately joined in fierce firefight. General mayhem and pandemonium prevailed for the next two minutes, which seemed like an eternity.

"Thank God Biff bullet proofed the carts. I'd be a dead duck!" Serge sighed.

The terrorists continued firing, making the way slowly under fire to the control door, never losing sight of their ultimate goal, the A/C room.

Serge winged one Cuban in the shoulder, spinning him around. Serge continued firing prone from behind the cart. He saw the terrorist wince in pain, and heard him grunt amid the gunfire, but the terrorist kept firing despite his wound. He refused to go down. He had a mission to complete.

"Tough S.O.B!" Serge observed.

The racket of the intense, close encounter gun fight reverberated up and down the confined hallway, almost deafening. The smell of cordite and gunpowder choked the air in its haze. With bullets flying everywhere, it was difficult because of the sheer numbers being fired and ricocheting around, to get off an accurate shot by friend or foe. Even expert marksmen found it impossible to sight their target without a serious risk of being hit in the hailstorm of bullets coming from everywhere. There were a lot of near misses.

A bullet came wheezing by, nicking Serge's ear. Blood smattered the side of his face and the service cart. In a 'matter of fact' manner, Serge changed clips and continued firing, ignoring his injury.

The terrorists finally reached the door despite the barrage. Luis inserted the key while the Cubans continued firing, almost emptying their extended clips of their automatic rifles.

The heavy door swung open. Luis stepped in, pulling the wounded man with him while his compatriot sent one final burst of automatic fire in Serge's direction.

A sudden quiet fell as the gunfire ceased... Serge heard the heavy control room door slam shut with a bang, followed by the loud click of an industrial lock echoing down the hallway.

"Oh my God!..." Serge sighed.

CHAPTER FORTY TWO
BIENVENIDOS — SUNDAY 10:30 AM

The big steel door slammed loudly behind them. They had reached their final destination. They sighed with relief. They made it!

They were safely inside the dark A/C control room. Luis probed for the light switch, so they could quickly complete their deadly plot. By the time the gunmen in the hallway broke down the steel door, the canister of Anthrax would be aero soled into the stadium's ventilation system. No one could stop them now. Mission accomplished!

Luis switched on the overhead fluorescent lights. The sudden illumination impaired their vision momentarily When their eyes adjusted to the light, they were absolutely startled!

"Bienvenidos. Manos ariba! A la pared!"

"Welcome. Hands up! Up against the wall!"

Biff Roberts commanded.

The shocked terrorists were confronted by a small platoon of commandos in helmets and flack jackets, pointing twenty M-16 semi-automatic rifles directly at them. The platoon stood behind a hip high concrete barricade, blocking access to the stadium's ventilation control panel.

They terrorists had only two choices. Surrender or die!

The terrorists froze. Astonished, dropping their weapons. This dramatic, incredible turn of events absolutely stunned them!

Finally reaching their destination, only to fail!

"How could the Americans possibly have known?"

A puzzled, amazed expression swept across their faces. Their body language said it all, "Our mission failed!"

Biff grinned in triumph. Nothing more needed to be said.

www.ingramcontent.com/pod-product-compliance
Lightning Source LLC
Chambersburg PA
CBHW050932120626
46552CB00001B/169